Jump, Gig, and Rig

Day Jobs are Hell

Daniel Jose Ruiz

Android Press

Published by Android Press
Eugene, Oregon
www.android-press.com

ISBN: 978-1958121733

Contents

PUDDLE-JUMP

1

Nathan Olamina would kill himself four times, an unlucky number considering the odds. Each time he should have felt something. Maybe some understanding that what he was doing was wrong, some revelation of spiritual importance. All that he felt was how odd it was to see himself lying dead on the floor. All that he could think was it was better this way.

It was the current of the moment before, not after, that Nathan had to swim against. Once it was done, it was done, and there was no need to reflect or justify. It was the moment before when the memories, the memories of the possibilities, would consume him. Each time, before he made blade pierce flesh and sever nerve, the memories of a life not lived and a life endured would rush into him.

I am not this man. I was never this man. I never wanted to be this man.

The first death was the easiest. The DNA was identical. The name was identical. The same sloped back and subtle acne scars hidden by mocha skin. The first time, the other Nathan clearly had suffered some accident. His once noble nose was half gone, replaced with a poor attempt at plastic surgery. He was obese, his typically strong jawline swallowed by several chins. His home was desolate, ragged. It was a grave for the living.

It was the first time Nathan had jumped to an Earth where he existed, and to see himself in such a sad state, he cursed the betrayal of probability. Sad Nathan should have noticed the other. Nathan stalked forward, awkwardly avoiding the dirty dishes, the half-empty containers, the vermin. Nathan's progress was slow, loud. Sad Nathan did not notice, too focused on the glowing screen of his console.

On this Earth, Sad Nathan was a military man, just like Nathan. *Real Nathan*, he thought. Sad Nathan was not an officer, not elevated to a specialized unit. On this Earth, Sad Nathan stayed a grunt, and so he suffered like one. At least Sad Nathan managed to learn to read and use a console. Maybe the Corps here were more focused on recycling injured soldiers. Something bad happened, and Nathan could only run through his own memory of close calls to see if maybe in this place, he stepped left instead of right and took a blast to the face.

I survived. I survived and survived whole. I will always carry that guilt.

I was in Constanti. The flybys had blown out most of the buildings ahead of us. I was deaf in my left ear from a homemade mortar. Another Contractor-Corp was half a kilm west of us, pushing on the same objective. We had no orders to engage, but that meant nothing when in the scrum. We needed to run if we were going to make it without bloodshed.

Boom. Click. Boom. Whine. Haze. Another mortar, not homemade. It killed—what was his name? Rosales? I don't remember anymore. It killed him, but his meat-suit blocked most of the shrapnel. I was down but not out. Someone got me to my feet. Someone got me running.

It was better than home. I remember saying that to myself, every quiet time. Didn't matter how many people died, didn't matter the pain. I was eating twice a day, sometimes to my fill. It was in the Contractors that I can remember first eating to the point that I stopped wanting to eat. Such a strange sensation. It was easy to love that feeling. It was easy to drown it, but I knew Mama would raise hell if I did it too much. It wasn't smart, she'd say.

"World is full of people who are strong, but that just means a back that won't break quick. You wanna survive? Be smart," Mama would say, every day before we went out to the Scrap Yard. Every day we were not sure we'd come back with anything to show for it.

It was so hard to not eat until it all came back up again. It felt like the world was ok for a few minutes. It felt like I had control over my own life.

We were in the mess hall. Rosales, if that was his name. Elahi. Nishimura. Tamayo. Patel. Richards. Ngozi. They were my friends. They told us not to have friends. They told us not to get attached. Trueborn Corpfolk understand the Corp is what matters, not us. We didn't believe them. We didn't care. We were all sixteen, maybe seventeen at the oldest. All Yardies and Farmies. We lived long enough to get here, and now we were trying to live long enough to maybe get a job somewhere else when it was over.

Rosales died in that blast. Patel died a few weeks before. Richards two days later. Drone strike, right in the chest. He was smiling too, right before he saw the incoming. Bright blue eyes, shining out in the smoke. Ngozi died from the Dust. Her breather was ruptured, and a storm hit us hard, and she choked there, unable to keep it out. Not sure what happened to Nishimura. We rotated home after that. Not sure where he went. Elahi and Tamayo, I went with them to the new training. They said we showed promise.

Was that it? Is Rosales alive here? Was it someone else? Did Elahi take it? She was smaller, most of the blast would have gone over her, right into me. Did it get no one? Did we all make it into that building?

No, likely not.

Your friends are dead or alive, and it doesn't matter right now. I am alive right now.

I am alive right now.

Nathan fought himself back into the present, into reality. Sad Nathan was still typing away, still entranced by the glow. It was the smell that shook Nathan. He knew his own odor, the reek of his hot sweat on dirty skin, of heavy bowel movements, of teeth left uncleaned for a week. He had survived enough war to know how he smelled.

But here, the smell was different. It was pungent, deep in the walls and the cheap plastic, but it was sharper, almost synthetic. It did not smell like war and it did not smell like poverty. It smelled like a resigned acceptance of irrelevance.

Nathan's training told him to strike now, strike while the target was distracted, strike while the risk of failure was at its lowest. Infiltrator training was not much different than standard Reconnaissance training in the Contractor-Corps. Think like the predator you are, with surprise, brutality, speed. Nathan's eyes locked on the folds of skin behind the man's head, but then they drifted to the floor.

Half-eaten rations on the ground, hollowed out by insects. Dozens upon dozens of thin plastic bags full of whatever passed for the local potato chip. Here, yams seemed to be the dominant crop for disposable food. A rectangular box full of what looked like ramen noodles. He had not seen a pizza on this Earth. What a pity. Nathan looked at the crumbs of gluttony and the memories surged again.

My Mama raised me better than this.

I would never disrespect my home like this. Hovel or castle, a home is a home. Mama used to say that. She was always so tired, but every day, she swept the dust and ash out of the room. Every day, I would help her clean the filters from our masks. I would sit with her and repair them with whatever we could find. Mostly old sponges, sometimes grounded up charcoal from fire pits. Lots of tape, even old gum. Whatever kept the worst of it out.

One day, she was so happy. She found a whole meter of rubber tubing with almost no holes in it. We spent hours, forgoing sleep, to carefully cut it down, use it to line the doorway. Hours of work, but it saved us hours of our lives later. Not as much got through the door after that. When Mama was so tired that she came home and immediately went to sleep, she did not even need to beat the rugs too hard to make it workable. She barely coughed. I swept that night, even with my back hurting from carrying scrap.

I wasn't perfect though. I ate her ration once. I was so hungry. She cried so hard. I was maybe six, seven? I don't remember, but I was hungry. She didn't raise her voice, and she didn't hit me, but I knew she was just as hungry, and I felt so ashamed. I nearly passed out the next week since I kept taking some of my protein sticks and mixing it in with hers, so she wouldn't notice. I made up stories about earning some extra for her.

I wonder if she knew I was lying? I don't think she did. I don't think she would have let me give her some of mine. I think she would have given me more if she knew. She was like that.

I wonder what his Mama was like. She wasn't like mine. No. She couldn't have been.

Mama could have gone mean. I wouldn't have blamed her. Mama could have beat me for taking her food. Mama could have sold me to someone that needed a lanky kid that knew how to strip copper out of a building. Mama could have sold me to one of the Executives as a personal toy or a moving target. Mama could have worked less for more without me.

Maybe his Mama was just too tired to care. Maybe his Mama died early.

I am not there anymore. I am here. I am here.

Nathan switched back. He looked at the man, the man that didn't know death was so close. Nathan took the blade—a standard blade of sharpened ceramic that cost far more than the home he had shared with his Mama—and he buried it between two folds of skin.

The rattle. The death. The smell became worse. It was over.

Judging by the hovel, the garbage, the stench of it all, Nathan thought it was a mercy. Then he stopped thinking about Sad Nathan entirely.

Nathan replaced Sad Nathan at the desk, covered in laminated code-books and a large console with several screens. He inserted the data-worm. The console still used a form of USB, so the small machine was able to quickly adapt and connect. Nathan smiled as the program went to work. He sat there, next to the still warm corpse of himself, mindlessly thumbing through the files on the chaotic desk and munching on the roasted legumes.

That first death, Nathan was there for three days before returning from the Puddle. He managed to catch another team's return window and saved his Corp from having to open it again for him later.

Nathan never found out what data he stole, but it came with a bonus. The data-worm worked too fast to consciously track any of it, but it did not matter to Nathan. That Earth also had a robust internet infrastructure, so the data-worm filled several Zetabyte storage drives. Nathan would not have to jump for some time after, but he did anyway. He always wanted to jump.

At least Sad Nathan's Earth had cows, real meat in their food, and the local burger chain was delicious. In his youth, Nathan would have giggled at seeing Big Belly Burgers on the West Coast of North Americci, but he had seen much stranger things. It was his homecoming ritual to grab a burger, or closest replacement, before a Jump, just in case.

The Mirrors were perilous. The openings were localized to the size of the object that initially entered with only a slight percent increase due to slippage. If you didn't position yourself correctly, you'd return missing something. Thankfully, most teams dragged through a few heavy cryo-cabinets, useful for transporting valuable material, and that made it easy to find a way home if you couldn't find your own seam.

To Nathan, Jumping between alternate realities felt like stepping into an ice bath that was also on fire. The sub-atomic veil between realities, between causality, is empty of warmth, but when experiencing that extreme level of cold, it burns. It is the nerves dying. His first time, if not for the sheer instinct to stumble away from such a sensation, and the help of essentially being flung through the damn thing, he would have frozen down to the molecule. Absolute zero is an absolute terror, he often thought. His former teammate, Octavia, would begin each jump with the same mantra: *We are separated from an infinite expanse of ourselves only by a lack of movement.* He did not understand this, but then his focus was on hardware and software assets whereas she worked for a university to gather cultural capital. She was strange that way.

Nathan and Octavia were not close in a traditional sense, but they didn't need to be. They were teammates, and they Jumped together, but their romantic interludes were not neatly defined. Nathan was hired for his skill sets, and Octavia for hers. She could recite a hundred different poems from a dozen realities, and she could tell you by the syntax of a sentence what major literary figures did not exist in that work's timeline. During a Jump, she would find the closest institutionalized system of learning and begin to mine it. Plenty of Executives were keen on information like that.

Nathan didn't understand why. He knew damn well why his occupation existed, but with Octavia, he was not sure who was paying. He asked her about it over their pre-Jump drinks, just about every time.

"So, who actually signs your payment authorization?" Nathan asked, nursing the potato whisky in his glass.

"Do you ever know who does that?" Octavia countered.

"Fair. But really, who is spending a share of some-fifty billion dollars a second to see what versions of Shakespeare there might be?"

"An entity with far more foresight than you, I'd wager."

"That's not answering the question." Nathan took a deeper drink. There was not much to do before a giant machine ripped open the fabric of reality.

"Did you know that of the two-hundred and twenty realities mined that have English or a variant as a language, over one-hundred and four feature works written by PD James?"

"Who's that?"

"Clearly, an important figure. Imagine that, an infinite amount of possibilities, yet, by some strange probability, this woman wrote in most that we've found."

"That's the thing about Infinite, youngs, anything is possible. The things I've seen..."

"Don't call me youngs," Octavia snapped in her half playful, half serious way. "And yes, I understand infinite, but what is the probability of us randomly finding realities with such? She is far more important than perhaps our reality has given her. This is worth exploring. This is why we explore."

"I explore for a paycheck, and they explore for the paycheck," Nathan said. The Puddle was warming up. He could tell because Octavia's hair was now at a four-foot circumference. Once the static discharged, it'd fall back into place.

Nathan missed his old teammates. When the Jumps were far more random, you could end up anywhere, so teams stayed close. Now, it was all the same. Everyone had a different job. Every drone with a different task. This of course led to other troubles, but those were often profitable troubles for some.

2

I was never this way.

The second time that Nathan had to kill himself was the most uncomfortable. The home was located near El Pueblo, a common variant of the major urban center in the corner of North Americci. It was well-manicured, freshly painted with a sensible but eye-catching trim. Nathan could see the indentations in the soft grass of children's toys that were left out, but not so long as to permanently mar the plants. They were quiet specters that told a terrible story.

Nathan watched for hours, hidden in a large oak tree in the backyard. He watched and waited. The house was empty, save for himself. No, not him. Another Nathan. Someone else. A clockwork ghost.

Nathan descended, quietly removed the lock on the back door, and went inside, blade at the ready. The smell of lilac perfume still hung in the air, and he was forced to remember a strange, lilting laugh. On the wall, he saw his Military Ball picture, almost a replica of the one stowed in some forgotten storage device somewhere in his home. Marissa.

I was happy. It was the first time that I ever felt that way. That's not true. I was happy other times—a piece of chocolate, a day home from the Yard. It was the first time that I felt like the next day had the potential to be better. That was happiness: Tomorrow was going to be better.

I had returned from deployment in the CC. For the first time, I had an account at a Corp-Bank, and I had credit. It was a lot of firsts. First coffee shop. First time I ever spent money on something I did not need, but wanted. She was there, fixing one of the dispensers. Her hair was gold, actual gold plated. It was the style at the time. Her eyes were rubies. Her skin was copper. In her standard coveralls, she seemed out of a dream. Grease and silicon fluid. She smelled like burnt wiring.

I sat next to her, the sound of her drill almost soothing.

"I'll be here awhile. Probably best you sit somewhere else," she said.

"All the more reason for me to sit here then." I smiled. So did she.

"Hope you didn't use the machine on the left; the syrup to water ratio is always off." She looked at her tablet as she said this, adjusting the machine with a few swipes of her finger. It was beautiful to watch her read. She would teach me, eventually.

"I used the middle one," I said, at a loss for how to continue. Something about her eyes, the fire in them, the reflective sheen of the contacts, it made me feel bare, striped clean. "I wouldn't really know the difference, anyway."

"Farm or the Yard?" she asked. She put down her tools and before I could respond, she took my hands. Mine looked clumsy, ugly next to hers. "Yard, all day."

"Yeah, until sixteen. Then off to the Corps."

"GenEc? Apson? Micro?"

"GenEc. Bootown," I said. How many million others could say that? How many millions lived crammed in Bootown? GenEc was all there was. I was as common as common came.

She began to move her hands away, but once I felt that kiss of her skin, I could not so easily let it go. I gently took her hand and examined the palm.

"Yardie too, I see." Her palms were crossed with the same thin scars—carrying too much scrap, too much weight—the thin slices of tin and steel.

"Yeah, NeeNee. Micro."

"So how'd you get here?"

"Long story. Bad memories," she said as she took her hands away and put them back into her work.

"At least for now, I have the time to spend."

She looked at me, not so much smiling, but not making any other sign either. "There's a green space not far from here. Only a few credits for an hour. My shift ends at 2100."

It is not her. This was never our life. This could never have been our life. Places like this didn't exist where we're from. How is this possible? How does she exist and I exist yet the world exists like this?

He hadn't thought of Marissa in years. The Other Marissa was still beautiful. Had Nathan been younger, he may have fixated on it more, may have chased the memory farther, but he was a veteran, and he had become colder. Life had made him cold with purpose.

The second kill was his one-hundred and twelfth jump—only his thirty third to a human populated Earth. He had seen Bootown sit in a sea of smoldering ash, the neon glow of its radiation strangling the very stars. He had seen NeeNee exist as only a forest with trees taller than any he had seen before, a world entirely green. The air smelled so harsh, so cold and sharp that he kept his breather on at all times, even though all the readings came back clean. Even then, watching the sun rise over the trees, he thought of Marissa.

They had long since parted ways, but time meant nothing to memory.

He thought about that place, the city of trees. He called it forty-seven, his forty seventh jump. He thought about that world of green and thought about his first date with Marissa. He thought about how it all ended. He was there, in those trees of ghosts, because they ended. She never wanted him to Jump, but if she had stayed to see it, they could have run away to an emerald world. He would have done it.

Nathan took a deep breath, his shoulders suddenly heavy, and forced his eyes away from the picture. He looked at Family Nathan.

Family Nathan looked much the same as him, perhaps a little rounder, a little softer, but more or less the same. At least Family Nathan aged well. He was still in the Corps, but by the diplomas on the wall, he used it to go to school. In this Earth, the Corps gave you the chance to go to school. That sounded like Marissa's influence; she always wanted Nathan to learn more, not just what was needed but what could be found through learning. Judging by the medals, he was not too bad at soldiering, and judging by the photos of graduation and smiling cadets, he was not too bad at teaching.

Family Nathan looked older, but that wasn't a surprise. This Earth didn't have cellular regeneration. Nathan was forty-seven, but with the cell treatments, Nathan looked barely over thirty. It wasn't vanity that pushed Nathan to take the treatments. The Corps demanded all infiltrators take the treatments. When you were spending billions of credits, there was no point in trying to be frugal, particularly when all it took was one bad back to miss out on a trillion credit opportunity.

"They pay you what you're worth, and you know you're helping those shitbags when they pay you more. Far as I can tell, the more you make, the guiltier you are," Marissa said that, often. She said it more and more as they were closer and closer to being less. The memories crept back, slowly singing to Nathan. Sometimes they stampeded, and sometimes they simply rose up like the tides.

I did everything for her. I started all this for her. I wanted her to have more than we ever dreamed when hauling scrap.

Marissa sat on a collection of rags piled together, what passed for a couch. She was reading. If you could find them in the Yards, books were cheap. We had the money for a Vidscreen or a personal tablet, but Marissa never wanted to spend the credits. She'd rather go to the green spaces. We were saving for a new air purifier, two actually. One for Mama, one for us. Mama had her own room, and while she still worked the Yard, it was not in Bootown. We lived in a smaller, nicer Corps town, but there were always Yards. Junk wasn't going to get mined on its own. Marissa's folks were long since gone, but she and Mama got along well.

I was in training. I didn't know what for yet, but I was learning to read from Marissa, which surprised the officers. Mama had taught me Maths a long time ago, and I learned fast anyway. I read books right along with Marissa, but she could read faster than me. I was never gonna catch up with her.

I was in training, but I was already making twice what I did on deployment. They trained me with weapons, but not with drones. They taught me to fight alone, to kill quiet with just a piece of metal. They trained me with computers. They taught me to break systems, to search. They taught me to sur-

vive in green spaces. They taught me to endure cold and heat. They never told me what I was doing. I didn't care.

"I don't like it," Marissa said. She looked out the window. It was sealed tight. We almost never had to dust.

"I don't much like it either, but it pays good," I responded.

"I keep hearing about all these jobs opening up in places, but nobody talks about them and nobody who goes ever comes back. Something is happening."

"What kinda jobs?"

"Fabricators, stuff like that. They don't say where you'd go. The pay is legit though."

"So why not?"

"You know why," she said. "We never let these bastards win, Nathan. We never care more than the paycheck," and then she kissed me and we bundled the rags together for bed.

It was the next day, the Military Ball. It was how they told me that I was promoted; I was an officer now. My account tripled with a signing bonus. That meant deployment, but it did not matter. We danced. We were twenty-one, and we were making more money a month than either of our parents made in a decade. We made love and thought about the next day. We talked about going someplace different, even for just a few days. We talked about walking in green spaces as much as we wanted. We talked about having a real bed like the cinemas.

Then I jumped for the first time.

The suit did nothing to stop the cold. Four hundred kilos of rad-proof armor and still every part of me felt lost in some empty place. I thought of Marissa. It was a green space, a beautiful space. I knew she would love the world, hate how we ended up there. Hate me for being there. When the Jumps became public, Marissa did not take well to it.

I could never have had this. No. This could never have been our world. Places like this didn't exist when we were young. No, we had to make our world like this, and she could never accept that.

Nathan felt the pressure behind his eyes and the cold of metal in his hands, the only grounding he needed. He was real. The world he occupied may have been fake, an illusion, a bastard child of causality, but Nathan was real. He knew he was.

Family Nathan was hunched over a stack of papers, a pen in hand and a drink waiting. Nathan took a small breath, and forcing his hand to move faster than his mind, plunged the blade home.

Nathan tried not to stare at the photos of the children. They were a good-looking family. They looked like an advertisement for one of those illegal jump operations that promised an ideal reality with everything and anything you could want—propaganda for the lonely. Nathan tried not to stare at the photos as he searched for any physical credentials. The data-worm was having success on the family console, but the real prizes were in military systems, and it did not appear that Family Nathan had access to much. At least not at home. The academy would have more.

Nathan cleaned the scene. The auto-cauterization on his heated blade meant there was no blood, and most of the typical post-life bowel movement was contained by Family Nathan's pants. Nathan lifted himself up and hid the body in the trunk of the family conveyance. He was taught this was the best place to store the body of your alternate. He searched the home for any hidden or sensitive material, but he found none. He would have to go to the academy. This did not bother him.

Marissa and the kids arrived as he was leaving. He covered his face as best he could with a hat and his body with an oversized jacket. He fought the urge to run. He fought to stay awake in the present and not dream the possible pasts.

Stay awake. Stay awake.

"Love, I'm home," Ghost Marissa said. She's older than Nathan remembered her, more wear on the eyes, on the soul. Ghost Nathan stood, home from deployment and nursing a bruised but whole body. The two ghost children ran to greet their mother, and somewhere, Ghost Mama was singing as she made dinner. They had a real house, made of concrete and plastic and wood. There was green grass in the backyard, and the air didn't smell sterilized by a filter nor strangled in ash.

This is not a memory.

He kissed Older Marissa politely, fighting every natural urge to fall into the seduction of roads diverging in a forest, and he greeted the children kindly. He did not have children at home. Not anymore. They smiled at him.

Stay awake.

"Paba, can we all go to the park after dinner?" the Ghost Son said. He had Nathan's smile but Marissa's bearing.

"Did you get all your work done from school?" Ghost Nathan asked. *Imagine that, my kids going to school. Real Mama would never have thought that could happen, oh no.*

"Yes, but Mama needs to look it over before bed," the Ghost Daughter added. She looked just like Real Mama, except young and unbeaten by the world.

"Then I guess we'll go to the park," Ghost Nathan said, smiling in an impossibly paternal manner. There was music in the house, and Nathan thought he could smell baking flour. Real flour, not acorn dust. *No, this is not a memory, only a dream.*

You never had this. You never will. Accept it.

Nathan gave an excuse about work and disappeared. He did not return to Family's Nathan's place despite Older Marissa's constant phone calls. He managed some usable material from the academy, mostly schematics for experimental missile systems that were slightly more efficient than those at home, but it was something. While not in his usual repertoire, he stole several hundred number one songs as these would be valuable. This was before teams started including cultural excavators.

He also ordered himself a rather large and immediate life insurance policy on that Earth. He made sure it was executable before he jumped. He disposed of his vehicle with Family Nathan inside at the bottom of a canyon, his alternate in the driver's seat.

He blamed the delay on lack of usable intel. His bosses did not like him diverging from the schedule, but he made it in time, just not early. It was unavoidable, he said in response. It was not a highly profitable jump, but not all of them were. He had made enough money for the Corps.

3

Nathan had visited eight hundred and twenty-seven realities. He was one of the first infiltrators and the only survivor from the first generation. He held the world record for jumps, but only the company knew this as most of his jumps were not officially recorded. Not much surprised him, but he was getting old, tired, even with the cellular rejuvenation treatments. Old wasn't in the cells; it was in the mind.

He had visited so many realities that the two common outcomes of probability no longer frightened or amused him. First, at least ninety-nine percent of realities are devoid of humans. Whether it was a quirk in evolution, a particularly nasty pandemic, meteor strike, or most commonly, nuclear war, humanity excels at going extinct if all the variables for a habitable planet existed at all. The Puddle-Pilots were trained to navigate the infinite vibrations of choice, and they were quite adept at piloting to realities where humans still exist, but they were not easy to find. Nathan's company was not in the resource game, so they needed humans to still exist because technology was far more valuable than uranium or rhodium.

This led to the second common outcome: if humans existed, they had mostly followed a consistent technological progression, but there were often a few key advancements that each reality reached at different points.

In Nathan's third time killing himself, that Earth had yet to develop nanofabrication, cold fusion, or even cellular regeneration, but they did have complex neural uplinks, allowing for instantaneous communication, piloting, and data-download.

That version amused Nathan the most. It took him several days to find his alternate. Nathan was certain that each version of himself was drawn to military service, but in the infinite realms of himself, he was everything and anything, yet part of him still believed that maybe, just maybe, there was an order to it all.

Of all things, Nathan was a PE coach on this Earth. Nathan could not help but stifle a laugh to watch another version of himself bark on young men and women as they ran laps. Nathan was not a small man, but he was also not necessarily large, but in this world, he seemed a giant.

Being a PE coach was not ideal as Nathan relied on access to military and corporate systems, but in this reality, the valuable technology was available at any retail outlet. There was no need to kill his Other, but training dictated that he do it. He followed protocol and waited for his Other to return home.

When he entered the well-maintained but structurally cheap apartment, he found his ex-lover of many years waiting. It wasn't her of course, but then part of Nathan didn't care.

Eliza sat on the couch, confused as to why Nathan appeared much slimmer and younger and how he came through the front door when she had seen him napping in bed. Nathan paused, watching the movement of her eyes, the subtle ticks of her mouth when she was processing, when she knew that something was deeply wrong but had no real proof of it.

Some infiltrators take pleasure in being able to revisit their past, the possibilities of it. Some infiltrators go rogue and stay, living a life that they wished they had, living with choices they wished that they had made. Some infiltrators simply carouse with old lovers, just for the memory made flesh. Some infiltrators get revenge.

"What's wrong?" he asked nonchalantly.

"Nothing, I think. Just déjà vu," Eliza responded, her amber eyes revealing a constant spin of doubt and introspection.

"You know that ain't real. Probably just tired," Nathan said. He scanned the room for anything he could use to undermine her own sense of reality. He saw the prescription bottles on the small dining room table. Nathan had seen enough Earths to know that in most realities, pills were a cheap, middle class, disposable piece of chemical coping, necessary to live in a fundamentally broken world. "You take one too many today?"

"I don't think so. My back hasn't been too bad," she said.

"Well, just rest. Take a nap on the couch," Nathan said as he fixed himself a sandwich. She made some noncommittal noise but with a few gasps of pain, put her body horizontal. Nathan went to the back room to find his Other. In the hallway, a tiny table—far older, stronger, than the kitchen one—forced the deep pains to rise. Eliza's mother's antique table, the only commodity she ever treasured. Made of real hardwood, built by hands with metal tools. Ugly, beaten from age. Two candles were burning, lit not that long ago. Heavy wax stains where many candles had burned.

A hand-knitted bib. A picture of an ultrasound, late term. Nathan could see the rough shape of the nose, his nose. The slant of the forehead, Eliza's.

This is not my son. This is not my son. Please, God, don't make me remember him.

I am the first to admit that Eliza and I should never have gotten married. She was a Puddle-Pilot, something like a workplace romance. I was in quarantine and isolation so much, she would sit and talk to me. She'd been raised in some corn-factory town, a manager's kid. We were never going to work, not in the long haul. She was a true believer to both her God and the Corp, but then, nobody really got what we did.

She piloted the first recon drones that made sure each Jump led to a place we could land, we could breathe, and we could survive. She had seen Earths where there was nothing but broken rock caught in a slowly dying gravity well where the Earth used to be. She had seen Earths that weren't there at all, just empty space. She had seen Earths where the sun was cold, blue, and so massive that it took up the sky, and the gravity crushed the drone before it could return.

We would swap stories while I sat in quarantine on my solo trips. I had been jumping for fifteen years, and by that point, there weren't many of us first-timers left. I couldn't tell her what I saw, but I did anyway. She made time fly by.

"So once, I swear to the Unified God, the sky was permanently orange from the fires. A bright orange like you'd never seen. Not much else but fire and ash," Eliza said.

"What caused the fires?" I asked.

"Seemed like constant volcanic activity. Lava flows everywhere, but the drone did catch a few places with jungle so thick and green, it looked like an island of heaven in a sea of hell."

"You send any poor bastards there?"

"No. The Execs didn't think the soil samples were rich enough for the cost. Just another in a long line of dead places."

"I guess you've seen far more dead places than me. Nowadays, they only send me when there is a reason to go," I said. I had Jumped so much, been to so many places, I couldn't help but be fascinated by someone who had seen more.

"Most of the worlds are dead because they aren't real. They were never meant to be real." Eliza shrugged. Her belief didn't bother me I suppose. It was probably a reason why we'd never get to the end of the game, but I was still youngish, then. I thought things like that didn't matter. She loved the Unified God, and she believed in our work.

"Well, I've seen a place where they put fish on pizza, can you believe that?" I smiled. She laughed loudly at this. "Can you honestly believe that some poor Took actually puts fish on a pizza?"

"Now I know you're tellin tall tales." She grinned honest, wide and ugly. She placed her hand against the glass, and I couldn't help but put mine up there too.

"You pilots get a bad rep I think. Or maybe you're the exception," I said, hoping just once, they'd let me out early.

"Ha, well I'm a real pilot. The others just sit at consoles all day and type in numbers. Takes fifty of them three weeks to enter in one damn coordinate chain," she said proudly. "They'd crash a drone within seconds, let alone pilot three dozen at once."

"That's a big number," I said. "You're impressive."

We married quick, spending a lot of credit and vac—time in the newly restored Ancient City. They reconstructed it only a few years ago, and most of the world's great treasures were there, put back together as if nothing had ever touched them. A city resurrected from the dead to pretend that the world didn't *end once, and we just happened to restart it. We danced for hours on end, laughing and being young and dumb. We spent the nights tucked away together, never thinking.*

Then the monthly physical showed she was pregnant. Mama was long gone, but I knew she would have been happy. I was happy. We had a real home, in a real city, with a real yard and the dust storms were so much better. We had the best filters, but some days, we didn't even need them. The eco-restore engines were just beginning.

He came into the world a screaming red, and that red tint never really went away. Eliza said it was an old bloodline in her family. He loved to build. He loved to stack: toys, boxes, books. He wasn't even two and he could stack blocks into towers taller than him. He would push his tongue out when he thought, it took up his entire top lip in a flat, pink sign of contemplation. He cried so hard, shook every part of me, when they radiated him over and over, trying to save him.

Please, God, stop.

Nathan drew his blade by instinct, focusing his entire will onto the heated blade and its purpose. His purpose. He entered the backroom and found himself asleep. He buried the blade with less precision and more energy. He pierced several times. Dozens of times.

"Everything ok?" Eliza called out.

"Yeah, all good," Nathan responded, panting. He quickly wrapped the body in a sheet and found several large duffle bags. He went about the task, turning the blade up to high to prevent any unneeded drip. This was a first for him, but he knew that it was eventual. In the world of the infinite, everything is eventual. He placed the pieces of himself in the bags and shouldered them. There was some evidence left, a few drops of blood that escaped before cauterization, the tears in the sheets, the mattress. He could see signs of the deed. The safest way would be to burn the place down, Eliza included. Protocol dictated that he clean the scene.

Nathan carried the bags out of the bedroom, his eye on his ex-wife.

"What is all of that?"

"Just some junk to donate to work. Been meaning to clean out the closet," Nathan said as he made his way out of the home. "Don't worry, I'll be right back."

Nathan left, walking out the door and not coming back. She had once done that to him, and he felt the same way he did now. He had to focus on work.

Being a PE coach was not lucrative, but Coach Nathan at least had open lines of credit. Nathan went to all the stores, relying on the data-worm to analyze the products to determine which were the most advanced to bring back. Of course, this bankrupted Coach Nathan, but it would not matter.

The data-worm needed time to decode the neural up-links as the programming languages were advanced, and with the extra processing power of several human brains, the cyber-security was impressive. All of this was a goldmine. Nathan felt fortunate. This would help people. This would make the Puddle-Pilots even more accurate. This would push everything forward not by a step, but a leap.

After a week, the data-worm succeeded, and with the neural link fully unlocked, Nathan knew that he'd likely never have much trouble hacking through a system again. This jump bought him a new home, far away from the des-ignated urban centers, deep in the mountains, deep in the forest, away from the walking shadows of the world.

4

Back home on his Earth—or as the Priests of the Unified World would say, the True Earth—Nathan lived a good life, far better than average. He remembered the world before the Puddles when he was a scrapper, then a soldier, an operative, good at his job, but still just a pawn. The corporate factions had warred constantly, and the few legislative governments ignored it. The world had nuclear energy and computing, but not much else. It wasn't until trans-dimensional travel became possible that everything changed.

It was the key, the one true ingredient to peace. In over eighty-thousand recorded explorations, most of them unmanned, only one Earth that was not a direct causal off-shoot of Nathan's Earth had developed the technology. It was theoretically possible, and they had all the math and models they needed, but they were a world ruled by over two hundred nation states, and without the unity of resources required to exploit the technology, it remained a theory. Nathan knew how much the Puddles cost to build; he remembered the Corps choosing to ignore the cost. In one day, the concept of money ceased to exist, if only for this project. In real currency, each Puddle had to cost at least ten trillion.

They built five Puddles. They were magnificent to see. He had Jumped from them all. Each stood over a mile in the air and stretched out over three miles in length. They crackled with purple and blue lightning like gods of antiquity, and when the Puddle opened, there was the silkiest, most flawless black inside that swallowed any garish color. It was like praying at the foot of some impossible god when Nathan would approach a Puddle.

Nathan was there when the other Earth was found, when the data-worms discovered that these alternates were capable of Jumping if they tried. Nathan was a trusted member of the team, a survivor and productive. He had even met Chairsmen, allowed into their presence. The young remnant of Nathan wanted to kill them all, to avenge a childhood of misery, to avenge Mama, but then, Nathan wasn't young anymore. Nathan went into this dangerous Earth, even after the first infiltration team came back with all the valuable material.

Nathan went in carrying several suitcases of weaponized flu. He committed genocide by sitting in a chair and reading magazines in a language he did not speak save for the translator embedded into his nervous system, talking to the people he was killing. He liked to talk to people, liked hearing their stories. He told himself over and over, they weren't real. This was a dream. He couldn't think of them as real.

"My parents came over to Oceania after the Last War. They arrived on a boat with ten thousand people. Nothing but the clothes on their back," the Old Woman said.

"Impressive," Nathan said, honestly.

"Very. From nothing they built a life," she said, idly stirring her tea. "Anytime work gets frustrating, I just think of them and know I'm lucky."

"I know the feeling," Nathan said.

"What did your parents do?"

"Never knew my Daddy. He died before I was born. My Mama worked in a scrap yard, sometimes cleaning the fancy places when they were hiring or selling her stitch work."

"You come from hard-working stock, too. I could see it in your face, your hands," the Old Woman said.

"Thank ya, Ma'am. I try, every day."

"She must be proud of you."

My mother is dead and she doesn't know—can't know—what I do. My mother is dead, but she smiled at me before she went.

We were all still together. Marissa, Mama, and I. Things were getting cold with Marissa. She hated the idea of the Jumps, and so far, like everyone else, she didn't know about the worlds with people. The Corps only said that we could navigate to unoccupied Earths, places where humans never developed or died out long ago. I had a big legal contract that I didn't really understand and a tracker in my neck to keep me quiet. I had already been to one with humans, just one. Xeres conquered the Greeks in that one, and as I came to learn, that one was one of the "advancement points" that the Pilots would talk about. Seems like in the infinite world of causality, some moments mattered more than others, and that was one of them. I had killed four people there, stealing their identification cards to get something out of their computer systems as well as credits to eat. I told myself they looked like Manager assholes.

She knew that I was hiding something. She knew that I couldn't be honest. The Corp was watching me too close. Still, our life was as good as we had ever thought it would be, in ways we never had. Life was still what it was, and Mama couldn't fight off the life that she had lived forever.

"What did the doctor say?" I asked at dinner. I had just come back from a Jump to a mostly frozen Earth with little assets but untouched resources. An excavation team was already assembling by the time I made my way back.

"Oh, nothin. Nothin to worry," Mama said, stifling a cough. Marissa looked at her closely, a mask that I couldn't read.

"She needs to rest. Doctor says to keep her home," Marissa said.

"I'll be damned, stay at home. And what am I gonna do then?" Mama sneered.

"Rest. We'll get you a vid-screen. Watch something. Learn a hobby," I said. "You don't need to work anymore, Mama. Me and Mars got it."

"Ain't nobody so rich they can stop working, boy," Mama retorted. "Plus, I don't need no stories."

"Well, damn, Mama. Then you won the sweepstakes cause you are. Me and Mars bring home enough." I took her hand and smiled at her. "You don't need to work yourself to death anymore. You won."

"Because my Baby Duck be doing God knows what? You know I can't believe them lies they say about other planets. You doin something you know you ought not do!"

"Believe it, and finding these empty places full of birds and trees is gonna keep us like fat rats," I said proudly. "You know I hate the corp just like any Yardie should, but they pay real good." I showed them the transfer notification of my bonus for finding several design prototypes of what looked like fusion reactors, or as close as I could figure.

"No Corp is going to pay this kind of credits for trees and birds," Marissa said, watching me closely.

"For oil and uranium, they will," I said. Even then, I knew that she knew I was lying.

"Lord, that a lotta credit," Mama said, somewhat admitting defeat. "A week. I'll rest a week and then there is work to do!" she declared.

She didn't survive the week.

She went coughing hard. I could hear the bones crack under the weight. There was no room at the clinic, and even with my bonus, we couldn't afford the real hospital. She was at home, on a proper mattress. She held my hand and coughed red.

"Mama, I got some more medicine. It's supposed to help," I said, trying not to dampen her face with my tears.

"Take it back. Sell it. You'll need the cred," she said between coughs, a heavy wheeze. I probably shouldn't have let her talk. "Let me die cheap."

"Mama, please don't. Mama, what can I do?" I pleaded. We both knew. I didn't want to know, but we both knew.

"You keep doing what you doing. Keep building a life. Build a life for as many as you can. You a Yardie from Bootown, and now you a fancy soldier type." She stopped for a while, coughing, but with each cough, she held her finger up in her usual I ain't done talkin way. "Build a life for as many as you can."

The coughing continued until I administered the injection. It calmed the cough. It slowed her heart, until it stopped. She held my hand and smiled at me until the end, and I cried into her for hours.

Marissa was at work, and when came home, she could only hear the sobs. She didn't need to see. We paid for a collection team, and they took Mama away. Two men in dirty white clothes took Mama away forever.

I used my bonus to pay for a proper burial, her ashes placed inside a building with thousands of others. The Company even gave me a burial bonus, which pissed me off then. Now, at least it was some recognition, more than she ever got before. She wouldn't just be incinerated and recycled into some cheap insulation. It was just Marissa and me. Mama would have wanted a preacher, but I didn't care. I didn't need nobody telling me about her.

"She loved you, and she was the hardest working woman there was," Marissa said. She held my hand as I cried when the man took the box with her ashes and placed it into the cubby space. = Her name was written in gold lettering.

"She didn't have to die like this. If we could have afforded to take her to a better doctor, the ones with the machines, they could have seen this coming."

"We didn't have the credits, and your Mama was not about to let you go into debt for it."

"They could have fixed this easy as anything. She didn't have to die coughing. No Exec-kids ever die of Ash-Lung. No Exec ever dies at 40."

"I'm sorry, Nathan. I am. We did everything we could."

"I bet you there is a world out there with a machine that could have seen it and fixed it. One you could have at home." In my grief, I forgot about everything I signed. The tracker in my neck didn't.

"No such place here."

"But out there, maybe. If I could have found it first. If I could have been there and taken it..." I trailed off. My neck began to burn.

"Just dead rocks out there. You said it yourself, an infinite Earths, and no way of ever finding one with other people," she said, probing.

I was about to speak when my communicator went off. Priority message from the Corp. I was being deployed, immediately. By the time we left the grave building, a transport was waiting. I kissed Marissa goodbye.

I never saw her again.

Two months later, when I arrived home, her stuff was gone. She left me a letter, hand-written and everything. She knew. She knew and she wouldn't be with someone who let the Corps do to new worlds what they had once done to ours. She ended with: You used to hate them, and now you are them.

I am building our world.

"Very proud, I'd like to think," Nathan absently said, shaking off the memories. He clutched his briefcase tightly, drumming it for the reminder of the present. He needed to stay in the present.

Each airport, one canister was left behind, and by the time Nathan had Jumped back, they were already active. While viral weaponry was inherently a terrible idea as there was no way to ensure that it would not wreak as much damage to yourself as to your enemy, it was a perfect weapon for pacification of another reality. All it took was a few well-placed canisters at major international airports, and within a few months, the planet was ready for resource acquisition.

Nathan received a nice bonus, but as his company was not in the resource game, it was more of a pittance to acknowledge his part. Once everyone was sure the virus had burned itself out, crews went in from the Nigerian Puddle to start the process. The raw resources taken from that planet allowed Nathan's Earth to colonize the Moon. Of course, it was not common knowledge that any of the Corps had these protocols, but it only took a simple lie to convince almost all: a global pandemic had driven humanity extinct in that world. Not even the workers really knew.

Most people would be upset to learn that as part of their reality's exploration, such a thing was on the table, or in Nathan's case as an infiltrator, that he murdered himself and many others without much qualm. The average citizen was convinced that all the realities visited were barren of human life, and so with infinite realities to mine, there was no moral issue in utilizing the natural resources of a humanless planet. The average person doesn't want to know either.

Nathan understood this. He understood that no one wants to see how the protein slurry is made, so long as it is plentiful, and it was all plentiful. No one cares as long as everything works.

5

Nathan sat with Octavia at a café.

"How old are you, really?" Octavia asked as they sipped their coffee.

"Today? sixty-three, I think. Mama was never real clear on my exact birthday. The day, sure, but not the year. I don't think she remembered to be honest."

"My God. The treatments really do work. Do you know on what Earth we discovered them?"

"Despite the popular rumor, I have not been on every Jump. It wasn't one of mine," Nathan quipped.

He enjoyed watching the city street hum. This was the first time that he had taken Octavia to a place that held any memory for him. They did not talk about their past. They talked about work and what could be.

"At some point, we may find an Earth that was actually colonized by other intelligent species, perhaps a spacefaring one. How marvelous would that be?" Octavia mused. She did that often.

"So long as it gives us something we need."

"Hard to think of it at this point. Any advancements are simply too fantastic to believe, theoretically true or otherwise."

"I am sure the idea of the Jumps are pretty out there. At least they were when I was a kid."

"Quite." Octavia sipped her coffee. The seeds and horticultural skills taken from an Earth that Nathan had visited. He thought it was mostly a dull place, but the food was good. "So few publishing houses print first-hand accounts of life before the Jumps. You should write one."

"I don't want to remember."

I did remember. I remember being hungry, the constant reminder that my body was trying to live. I remember the agony of trying to stop myself from eating a protein stick in one bite, to chew slowly, to fool the body into believing a lie. I remembered the salt in my own sweat, my own piss.

I remember waiting for the inevitable war to flare up again, for the city to rent itself apart from bombs that cost more than I had ever used or was likely to use. I remember hoping another part of town would be struck, only for more scrap, the extra pay, for maybe some valuables to hide from the foreman. I remember waiting and praying that I'd make it to sixteen, just so I could enlist in the Corps for two meals a day and something for Mama.

I remember beating another boy near to death for an extra protein stick because I was so hungry there was no God anymore. I remember wishing I could kill all the Exec-kids and take their food back to the block. I remember the look on my only friend's face when he'd come back from a foreman's private dinner, pockets full and eyes hollow. He killed himself in Basic, the moment they gave him a loaded gun. They told us to forget him. I didn't. I remember Tamir.

"What did they used to call this city?" Octavia asked, and Nathan focused himself back to where he was, not where he had been.

"Bootown," he replied, automatically.

"Such beautiful art. Most cities go for a more classic Romantic theme for their public art, but this is clearly more West African."

"It is beautiful now, yes." Nathan kept himself fixated on the images in front of him. They were so unlike the past, they kept it at bay. The memories could not creep forward if the present was so beyond what they could understand.

"You grew up here, before the Jumps?" Octavia asked. Nathan nodded. Octavia took his hand, much to Nathan's surprise. "Show me."

The two walked the streets.

"Imagine each of these fruit trees or hedges was a shanty, built outta whatever you could find. Mostly junk metal, canvas, old clothes, anything to keep out the dust," Nathan began. He walked up and took one of the sweet blood oranges from the trees and peeled it. "The buildings were more or less in the same places, but almost none had glass. Half of them were ripped up from the bombs. Only the strongest crews ran them, and still, the dust got in anyway."

"Where did you live? With the strongest group I can imagine," Octavia said, oddly proud. Nathan let his grip on her loosen for the moment.

"No, I lived with Mama in one of those shanties. We hauled scrap outta whatever buildings were left or at the Big Yard where the lake is now. Mama wanted us to live in peace. All of us, even the ones in the buildings, just wanted to live in peace, even if you had to kill to have it."

"Seems impossible to imagine now. What was it like?"

"Constant. Always grit in your nose, your eyes," Nathan said, his mind drifting back.

It was my seventh jump. The Earth was warm, soft. No cities of any kind. No evidence of any hominid life. Hell, the folks in Bio-Recon seemed to think that there were no primates of any variety here. It was summer, and after a few days of scouting, I wanted to get clean.

The lake had water like silver. I removed all of my gear and swam, putting to use my training.

The water was cold, but I didn't care. I rose out from it and for the first time, I felt nothing on my skin that wasn't meant to be there. Just water, last vestiges of sweat. No grit. No dust. I took a deep breath and it was as if my lungs were not used to drawing in only the air. I wanted to live right there, in the water, for the rest of my life.

That's where I saw my first duck. I had only ever seen pictures of them before, the ones in the only book that Mama owned until Marissa came along. Mama would read it to me every night. Well, every night we weren't so tired that we didn't fall asleep the moment we went horizontal. She loved ducks. She told me stories about how when she was a girl, she lived near a pond, an actual standing body of water, and ducks would come and sit with her.

They are funny animals, awkward in their construction, but there was something sweet to them. Something simple, a simple need and a simple life. Watching the little ones go by, neat and ordered, shepherded by their parents, it looked like the way the world should have worked. How it did work in a lot of places.

I was so excited when I got home. I told Mama all about it, that I got to see a real duck. She smiled so big at me, laughed with a single tear gathering in her good eye. I wanted to take her there with Marissa and never go back.

I've wanted to live so many other places, at first. Now, I just want my world to live.

"On the bad days, the clouds would be taller than these buildings, and you'd suffocate in seconds if you were outside without a breather," Nathan said .

"We are truly doing beautiful work," Octavia said. She smiled wide.

"I saw them rebuild this place. I watched from one of the last Yards before they reconstituted it," Nathan said. Octavia squeezed his hand. "The constructor came in, same ones we use when we mine through the Puddle, and it slowly moved forward, spraying this grey goop every which way. Whatever the goop hit, it disappeared, melted away. Only took a day for the entire place to become this swamp of grey. Then the next, the goop started to move on its own, and suddenly there were trees, roads, buildings, all rising higher. Three days. It took them three days to turn twenty square kilms of slum into this."

"Nanofabrication and replication is a wonder. An absolute marvel of ingenuity," Octavia said as they continued their walk.

"I remember begging for a protein stick right here on that corner. Me and some odd hundred others. This was where the transit would drop off the foremen of the Yards," Nathan half-mumbled.

"You must think of me as such a spoiled child. You must think of most that way." Octavia brought Nathan close as she said this.

After some pause, Nathan said, "No, I am thankful. No one should know that life. No one needs to know it. There's no inherent strength in suffering."

"You know, the reason the others make jokes about your age is that I don't think any have met someone as old as you who wasn't a Shareholder or Board Member."

"I met the Chairmans of four different Corps, didya know that?" Nathan asked and Octavia's eyes held actual shock. "Twice. Once after my first Jump that brought back some new battery designs, and once after a solo Jump."

"Oh my. What were they like? I 've seen the vids and all that, but it can't capture the gravitas of actually seeing them in the flesh," Octavia said, still aghast. Meeting a Chairman was akin to meeting a deity. They were more rumors or myths than humans.

"First time, they were all three times my age, deep lines in the face, all smiles and soft skin. I could smell them before I could see them. Had hands softer than yours." Nathan laughed. "Second time, this was only a few years ago, same four. All of them looked younger than I do now."

Octavia gasped at this. "No, the cellular treatments can't be that effective, can they? They would all have to be well over a century old now. You're being facetious."

"Who knows how good they have it? If all of us kids from Bootown get parks and trees and schools and all the food we can eat, what do you think they get?"

"I suppose that is logical. Still, that is near immortality."

"Pays to be the boss, I guess."

"And this poses no moral quandary to you?" Octavia asked. Nathan assumed she asked because it presented one to her.

"The world will always have big rats and little rats. I suppose the only right thing to do is make sure the little ones have a good life, and so long as that happens, let the big ones have the impossible."

"The more chilling thought is, given causality, then there is a reality where the Companies keep all of these advancements to themselves, and Bootown is still what it was when you were a boy." Octavia chewed her lip. "This means there is a competing reality that is harvesting others, but with far less moral obligations. Chilling."

"Suppose that's true, but what are the odds of finding any specific reality?"

"Essentially a quintillion quintillion to the quintillion quintillionth power, and constantly growing. We do not have a number suitably large."

"So, then probably not an issue." Nathan laughed with not quite his usual mirth. They continued their walk. The way Octavia walked, didn't speak, he figured this would likely be their last outing outside of the Puddle.

6

Nathan had walked so many worlds, his enthusiasm for it waned. As he continued, he found less joy in the changes. His mind often drifted to the smaller alterations, the subtle ways in which a world is full or damning. Mostly what interested him was food.

In the earliest days, the only food was what you brought with you. Protein sticks, meal slurries, and maybe the odd piece of dried fruit-products. It was certainly better than the Contractor rations, but it was nothing like he would find in other realities.

Nathan had just finished a mission. His comm-upload—at this point entirely neural—reminded him to return to the extraction point within thirty-six hours. He had plenty of time. This Earth had more than enough high-speed transit, and their digital security was so little that he could easily charter a private plane within a minute. He calculated that he really had about twelve hours of leave time now, all on the clock.

He sat at a local franchise chain, its name some colloquialism that he did not get. The translators worked so well at this point that the word made logical sense to him, but the cultural nuance was lacking. It didn't matter. He sat alone at a table, a variety of small meals in front of him, and he began to eat.

He often mused that so many Earths discovered that frying edibles in some kind of oil was the cheapest, most efficient way to create delicious food, and here, it was fried broccoli. He enjoyed it, but this version of ketchup was far too heavy on the vinegar. Oddly enough, the mustard was heavier on the sugar. He did get a few looks for using mustard on his broccoli, but one of the commonalities of any Earth with a post-industrial society was that people typically did not bother to investigate much when it came to other people. Everyone was a stranger, and a strange one at that.

The patties in what they called a sandwich were made from reconstituted insect protein, not much different to the protein sticks of his upbringing. The taste brought back the sound of laughter.

I used to have friends. I used to share meals with friends.

"People really eat this? Like not just Execs, but normal people?" Elahi asked as she laughed. I never understood how such a small woman laughed so low that you felt it in your chest.

"I guess so. Doesn't seem like too shiny a place, and just about everybody here looks like they got a month's worth of food sitting on their bones," Tamayo said as she finished another bite. We had hamburgers at home, but they weren't real meat or bread but rather shaped protein. Only Execs had real meat.

"We need to come back before we Jump," I said.

"Why leave? Seems pretty easy livin here," Elahi said.

"That's a punishable offense," Peterson half-barked. He wasn't a Yardie or a Farmie. Technically, he was our officer in charge, but he was a low-level Executive's brat, so we didn't care much what he had to say. We fuckin hated him, and he

knew it. He was also so damn scared of everything that he knew the only thing that kept him alive was us.

"Just foolin," Elahi said. "I know for you, this is all dum-drum, but I ain't never tasted food like this."

"It is an interesting flavor," Peterson said. We never directly gave him a hard time, but he also knew that we really didn't care either. "Tamayo, how's the translation going?"

"Getting there. Definitely a variant of a Latin and Arabic base, but the system is having trouble tracking it," Tamayo said. She chewed loudly while typing on the small console in her lap. We instinctively clustered around her, blocking the view. It didn't seem like such a device would be out of place here, but it was not worth the risk.

"Well, get it clicking. I want to order more and I'd rather not just point and grunt." Elahi laughed.

"I want more of those nugget things," I said. "But how much do we have left?"

"Well, after our resource reallocation protocol…" Peterson began.

"You mean robbing a couple of people," I interrupted. Call things what they are. I remember thinking that: just call it what it is.

"Yes, so we have spent 21.5% of it for a single meal, one that seems economical in design, so I would say we should avoid using more local currency. Each time we, as you say "rob someone", we increase our chance of exposure," Peterson said.

"Do we even know what we are looking for?" Tamayo asked.

"We have the new cyber-investigation ports to test. We need to find consoles."

"Got it. Translators have a working proxy. No voice, but we can at least read things now." We all linked our translators *to Tamayo's console, and suddenly, the ocular HUDs could provide a translation of any written text.*

"Oh my god, this is made of goat. I am eating a goat." Elahi started pushing the food away. "Please don't tell my mother. She'd kill me."

"Whatever. Meat is meat," I said. "Besides, pretty sure that you weren't complaining ten seconds ago and whatever happens here doesn't count."

"Agreed," Tamayo said. Elahi looked at us, her meal, back to us, and finally to her meal.

"Well, she'd hit me harder if she saw me wasting food." Elahi laughed and continued eating.

"Finish up. We need to move." We all groaned at this, but Peterson was a Corp-man to the bone, and he needed the mission to come in on time and under budget. We fucking hated Company Men.

I remember the best part of a meal was when it was shared.

Nathan made his way to the closest airport and his data-worm did the rest. A small plane was waiting for him, the crew minimal. Nathan's data-worm had taken anything of worth, mostly several theoretical models for superconductor designs. At this point, it was becoming rote. The newest machines they gave him each Jump did more and more of the work.

As he flew, he watched out the window at the sea of trees below. This used to excite him, the idea of a tree, the idea of so many trees you had to call it a forest. It was so easy to take it for granted, and even now, he knew there was a whole crop of children growing up in his Earth that never, not once, had to doubt that there were so many trees in the world that you could get lost among them. He liked to think that this didn't make them spoiled or ungrateful. It meant that he did good work; it meant they were living life the way it was supposed to be.

The plane shook in turbulence, and below, Nathan watched the top of the trees sway in a hypnotic dance of wind. For a second, he could not help but smile.

We were so scared.

I remember struggling to breathe at the sight. I never thought there could be so many trees, let alone all in one place. They stretched up so high, it looked like they were all that held up the clear, blue sky. Even through the breather, you could smell that the air was different. I cradled my rifle and for a moment, I did not feel the weight of the exosuit.

"This isn't real. This can't be real," Tamayo said. She was on my right, doing the same thing as me. Whenever we were deep in the scrum, we knew to hold our rifles and wait. Shrill calls from some kind of avian ripped through the air, and we all assumed incoming positions.

"This ain't right, guys. This ain't right," Elahi muttered.

"Recon has assured us that no super-predators exist here. We are to investigate, gather samples, and exfiltrate within 48 hours," Evans said. He was our first commander, a soldier like us.

"I am still trying to warm up. I don't want to go through the muck again," I said. It was my first Jump, our first Jump. This was before the Puddle-Pilots were really pilots. They just turned on the damn things and sent drones in ahead to see if we could even survive.

"I don't want to die for some stupid rocks," Tamayo said.

"No one is dying. Get right with your nerves and let's move. Work to be done," Evans barked in that way that made you feel embarrassed but safe.

I remember digging, the weight of the suit crushing down. There were servos in the suit that made it lighter, but they quit after several hours of muck and pollen. We could barely move. I remember thinking I was going to die crushed inside my own suit or starve to death. It was Tamayo who led the charge.

"Whichever. Better chance without it," she said as she crawled her way to me. "Unfasten it. Get me out of this thing."

"Damnit, Tamayo. The servos will free themselves. We don't know what kind of crap is in the air here," Evans yelled. I didn't care. I began to unlock the mechanics that kept the suit together. After thirty minutes, Tamayo wiggled her way free. She sat on the ground, took several deep breaths, then let out a scream.

"Damn! It feels good here!" she shouted. It did not take long before we were all out of our exosuits, except for Evans. We tried to clean the servos as best we could, but they were jammed. The best we could do is prop him up against a tree.

We continued our mission, setting up geological survey equipment, sending out a swarm of recon drones, and taking various fauna samples. The atmosphere was slightly heavier in Nitrogen than our Earth, so we weren't quite at our best. We were slowly being poisoned, but it was a giddy experience.

"You've got to see these things. They are that, that, I dunno, that fuzzy," I said, my head caught in some cloud of warmth and numbness. They were some kind of insects, far different than I had seen. The only bugs I ever saw on the regular were lice and slumkites—large armored, flying beetles that ate just about anything but were toxic to eat. These new insects were delicate things, no longer than my thumb, wings of a shimmering blue and green.

"They are like tiny fairies, aren't they?" Elahi said, giggling like a drum at revelry. She put her hand out and several landed, and she fell to the ground laughing hysterically.

"We should take some back. For science. For science," Tamayo said as she chased them with a specimen jar.

"She's always right, but this time she's completely right," I said as I fumbled for another jar.

We spent the better part of the day chasing these creatures, combat gear clanging against us awkwardly. There were only a few negligent discharges before Tamayo got us clear enough to put our rifles down as we chased the bugs.

Luckily, most of our gear was automated, so we were still technically doing our job. For all three of us, it felt like being children, the way children should be. Growing up in Yards or Farms, there was no play. Since the day you could sort, you had a job. You didn't want to run unless you had to because each intake of air was risking death. We were running and laughing and joking, and some of it was the nitrogen, but most of it was not.

As the sun set, we watched the sky turn to a dark purple before a total black—a sunset with no electric orange and sickly green. Then we went back to Evans. He was still alive, measuring his breath as the weight of the suit closed in on him. The frames around the suit were supposed to keep this from happening, but also the servos were supposed to keep working. Tamayo rigged up our helmets to pump out some clean air, so we slept with our heads in the helmets, a little more sane, a little less poisoned.

Evans died in the night. The support frame finally pushed too deep into his chest, and he suffocated. We were still alive, and we still had the mission. He just had to stay in the damn suit, but he was too used to doing what he was told. I told myself I'd get out before that happened to me.

"Burn so bright that dust can't hide you," Tamayo said, a Contractor's goodbye, and then she took command. We finished our work.

We chased the little fairies again for a few hours. The equipment was done with most of its tests, and we began to pack it all up. It was easier to leave the material behind and take the data-chips instead, carefully protected in a hundred kilo box, just in case the Jump back was hard. Elahi got all of our suits working again, at least enough to make a few steps. We loaded up Evans on the gurney, and we walked back to the Puddle. This was before para-causal-string mechanics were discovered, so the Puddles only opened at prescribed times. You were either there or you weren't. We would lose Tamayo that way, many jumps later.

I like to think she found her own slice of probability and decided to stay.

Nathan thought about the times that he wanted to stay. He had found plenty of places, and it was the early days that were hardest. Before his world turned, before Bootown became something else, it was hard to return to his Earth. It didn't matter anymore. His world was his, and it was beautiful now.

He approached the Puddle zone and waited. Octavia was already there, a little perturbed. The biologist and geologist were en route as well, all chatter. Octavia and Nathan said little once through the Puddle. There wasn't much to say, and they knew it. They were ghosts walking in someone's dream world, and there was no reason to pretend that ghosts can hold anything.

With the team assembled, they all donned the Jump-Suits, a heavy nano-fiber suit that could withstand the chill for at least three seconds. Most of the younger ones complained about the cold. Nathan remembered having to wear a space-suit inside of another spacesuit inside of a personal tank, and even then, the chill went deep into the blood.

"Old-Clock, what's the jump count, really?" The geologist said. Nathan did not remember her name, Wa'thiongo maybe.

"More than you," Nathan responded, the same way he always did.

"Come on, tell us. There's a bet going around."

"Tell me the number to beat and promise me half, and then we can talk."

"It's just for a lark. No credit on the line."

"Then the honest answer is more than you," Nathan said. Octavia snickered at this slightly, giving Nathan a half-smile. "We all here?"

Nathan activated his beacon, and the air ten meters ahead of them seemed to harden. It was not quite a mirror, just a massive section of the horizon suddenly froze as if it was replaced by a perfect image of what was there several seconds ago. Birds with wings in mid-beat, leaves frozen in their descent. They approached, and each carefully scanned the picture for the subtle imperfections, the almost razor thin scars where they had first entered. Each took their mark, secured the little equipment they had brought, and walked out of the dream.

Nathan was glad to be going home. Octavia was not.

7

Nathan sat with Octavia in their usual café, only a few minutes by hyper-train to the transit hub where everyone was shuttled to their assignments. Octavia was off-rotation, but Nathan had a solo Jump scheduled. He did not care where. He only hoped for something that would save a life. Octavia looked around the room, ordered nothing, and started talking in a low voice.

"Do you ever stop to think, I mean truly ponder, why they did it?" Octavia asked, her voice low and her posture uncharacteristically paranoid.

"Not anymore. I used to," Nathan said, drinking his coffee.

"It seems almost illogical. Create a beautiful world for the benefit of humanity when before, they were happy with the way the world was," she continued. Nathan knew where this was going. He knew that tone, the tone someone takes when they are going to say something that is honest, that is real, that scares them.

I've heard this kinda tone fore. It means she's leaving. It means a decision has been made, and I can either get with it or get going.

I wasn't a slice of samosa after he died. I never much cared for the bottle or the synth-dopa, but after it happened, I didn't know what else to do. It didn't make anything go away. Still had the memories. Still could feel his tiny hand gripping my finger, gripping as hard as I ever felt, and then feeling that grip relax. Feeling the warmth fade. I still could feel it, and no matter what I did, it didn't matter. All the junk did was keep me from putting my own blade through my neck. All it did was make me chemically incapable of acknowledging everything. Including Eliza.

She soldiered on better than me, at first. She cleaned up after I was sick. She tried to talk to me. We cried together sometimes. She handled all the bureaucratic nightmares designed to remind you that you were still alive because the afterlife couldn't treat death in such a mundane, cold way. She even went to work, driving drones in beautiful places or sometimes ugly places with profitable resources. I didn't go to work, not at first. I sat at home and held one of his sleepers. I held it and cried into it until his smell was gone and there was nothing left but the stale, acrid scent of my breath infused into it.

She tried. She really did. She hired some school kid to come talk to me about it. I didn't say much. Didn't even let the kid say the name. She tried to convince me that it could get better, it could become bearable, if we tried together. She tried to tell me God had a plan. I could only go back to work.

Part of it was the hope that maybe I'd find the world where he didn't die or never had the gene or the gene never activated. I dreamed I could find that alternate, blessed version of myself and remove him, take the boy back with me. I looked into the back-room vendors for a transport kit that could sustain life and survive the trip. I went on every Jump I could, and still, it did not matter.

I was gone for six months, thirty Jumps. Hell, the bosses only let me to see if that many Jumps would kill someone. When I came back, Eliza's things were gone, but she was there, waiting for me. She wasn't the type to just leave.

"We could have done this together," she said.

"I can't do it," I said.

"If I can't do it with you, then I can't do it here." She looked at me with such anger and pity. "We serve the True God, and if he decided we don't get a baby boy, then that's how it is. But our life isn't over, and that doesn't mean forget, but it does mean we can try to live a real life."

"I don't know how to not hate everything in this world now," I said. Even the empty walls and empty rooms made me think of the hospital. Made me think of the empty boxes where we place what was left of our family.

"You can't think you're in more pain than me. You can't think I haven't wanted to end this whole place."

"Never said you didn't."

"You never said anything."

And with that, she walked away, papers on the vid-screen waiting for a thumb print. I didn't bother reading it, just imprinted and went to sleep.

I never said anything because I didn't know how to say it. How do you tell someone that you're positive that God is either dead or impossibly cruel? Maybe I had to do it. Maybe I had to fix the world because no one was going to fix it for me.

I still can't say much. I don't know how.

Octavia looked around again and placed a small machine on the table before activating it and hiding it under a napkin. Nathan's neck tingled as the neural implant was smothered. His contact-HUD died and he had to see the world the way he was born to see it.

"No one can hear us," she said quietly.

"Where did you get that?" Nathan asked.

"Least of our concerns," she said and then leaned in. "It does not make any logical sense. The Execs murdered this world to be kings and queens of slums, and then suddenly decide to remake the world. That is contrary to human history, from a thousand different histories."

"Well, maybe we are just lucky. I mean, by the numbers, one world would do it this way, " Nathan retorted. He did not like where this was going.

"And the odds of it are so small that it is again illogical to assume it would be us."

"Count your blessings."

"No, something else is going on. The powerful do not share resources unless they are sure that they will amass more power. This is human nature."

"Maybe we're the first to figure out a better way. Somebody has to be first."

"Yes, but not us. There is no historical, religious, or philosophical precedent in our world for this. We've visited dozens that were far more likely to reach this understanding, and most of them were still marred by inequity that almost rivaled our own."

"Maybe the whole Unified God thing isn't so crazy?" Nathan said, trying to lighten the mood. Octavia was not a fan, ignoring his attempt at playful banter.

"Focus, Nathan. Focus." She looked around again and pulled him so close that Nathan's unshaven face marred Octavia's. "What if they made this world a paradise so no one would ask what they did to other worlds?"

"Now you are getting a bit looped, Tav," Nathan said as he tried to pull away, but she held him tighter.

"You said it yourself, they haven't aged, actually becoming younger. It is reasonable to assume that they have achieved some of form of immortality, a godlike attribute, and what then do humans who fancy themselves as gods do? They create and enslave. What if each Exec has their own world, built any way they like, with any people they like? What if the cost of this world is the total bondage of dozens, hundreds, of others?"

"Calm down, Tav. This kind of talk gets people hurt." It was exactly the kind of talk that Nathan knew could not be tolerated. Octavia did not know about many of his Jumps. She did not need to know. Progress was what mattered.

"I must find the truth. I must. I cannot be part of a machine that turns others' worlds into what this used to be. I cannot," she said. She kissed his cheek deeply. "I need you with me on this. I need to know that I can trust you."

"What are you going to do?" Nathan asked.

"Get all the information that I can. I have leverage on a few pilots. I can get the data files. I will look through it all."

"So what do you need me to do?"

"Protect me when it starts to go bad. Help me get any information out to others. Tell me about your classified Jumps. You are the only one who knows what the early jumps were. You are a legend, and others will listen to you." She kissed him again and held his hands tightly. Nathan sat in thought. He looked into her eyes and found nothing there worth the rest of the world.

"I won't help you," he said as flat as his voice could manage. "I won't tell them what you're doing. I won't get in your way. But I won't help you with this."

"Why? Nathan, I need you. This is important. This is maybe the most important endeavor you could ever do."

"No, it isn't. Nothing ever will be again," Nathan said and stood from his seat. "This world is the best of any world. Whatever the cost, this world, our world, is worth it."

"You know better than anyone what a hellish world run by them looks like."

"That's right. That's exactly right," Nathan said before walking away, stopping only to add: "Be careful."

"So when did the Old Clock become a company man?"

Nathan left the café. Octavia left the service shortly after. He never heard from her again, never heard anything. As far as anyone knew, she used her savings to simply live a quiet life somewhere far away. Occasionally, Nathan would think of finding her, of seeing how it all went, but then there was no reason to. The world was what it was, and the past was what it was. If she really did try, she was probably gone.

Nathan Jumped. He went alone now. A new, covert Puddle had been built deep in the Asiatic Steppe, only large enough to send a few scouting vehicles at most. It spent most of its time open surveying worlds, logging their exact coordinates before moving on. With the 70% efficiency solar panels, the cost was minimal. Nathan knew it was just the natural progression of the technology. Eventually, there would be Puddles that could fit in a closet or even the palm of a hand. For all he knew, the Chairmen all had personal Puddles.

They sent Nathan when they needed something. He wasn't recon anymore, he was acquisition. On one Earth, it was a theorem, paracausal weaponry. The recon drones had managed to find mention of it, but the actual theorem was nowhere to be found. The full data was somewhere, likely in a hardened system. It was also an Earth that was a true off-shoot of his own, the first that he had ever seen. It was much the same, perhaps a bit less developed. They had Puddle technology, but not the resources or will to fully utilize it. Typical protocol would be to simply annihilate it, but then, an off-shoot would have the best technologies to harvest.

Nathan went in, starting with the obvious. If he was alive and in the service, he would have access. He found the last listed address, but he also found his death certificate: KIA. Here, the nation-states seized control and were at a near constant brush-war over the resources to utilize the Puddles. This slowed them down. Still, protocol dictated that he find his former residence and see if there were any useful means.

It was a small home, well-kept despite the conditions. There was no eco-restoration tech, so he had to wear a breather. Nathan made his way inside the home and began the search. There were almost no pictures on the walls. Then he remembered that this was a true variation of his own life, and in his own life, he never had anything on the walls that didn't keep the dust out. Clearly, in this world, he was still fortunate enough to have a real house with walls, a roof, and several rooms.

In the corner of the main room, there was that same damn table. Old, scarred, and haunting. The candles were there but not burning. A large framed photograph. It was a picture of Nathan, one he never took. Next to it was one of a teenage boy, with strong features. He had a dazzling smile and wild hair. He had a few scars that looked more from trouble than carelessness. He had the stance of a fighter, a scrapper of a boy that the world had made hard. Maybe Nathan had made him hard. The flood came.

I never had a boy like this. I never had a young man. I never got the chance.

I found a small room, a bed, posters of various media acts, and of course, a console. I was dead in this place, too. I was dead and buried, and I was searching for anything that could help me find whatever use that Earth had for me. There was a slight stink that I never encountered before, but I focused on the data-worm as it did its work. It found nothing, and I went to work the old way. It was refreshing.

Under the mattress, there was a torn picture. It was me, Eliza, and a little boy. My little boy. He must have been ten, maybe eleven. I dropped the photograph like it burned, and it did. I stared at it on the ground, hoping the distance would make it less real. The scent grew stronger, and I felt the air warp as another entity moved throughout the space. Someone else was in the room.

"Dad?" the kid asked, his hand grasping at his mouth as if trying to catch the word. "This is a mental break. Got it," he said more to himself. My training told me to move quick, draw the blade while in motion. My training should have kept this from happening, but damn, the kid was quiet. Maybe I was starting to get old.

"Baby Duck?" I said, which I knew was a mistake. I would have liked to say that it was my training, rely on this kid's Cog-Dis and play on it, but I think that would be lying to myself. I don't lie to myself.

"This isn't real. It can't be real," the kid said. "You're dead. You're in a box in the ground. You've been dead for ten years. You died and I buried you and I cried over your box. I just went there last week." He started to pick up speed in his voice, which is when I knew that his mind was starting to tear itself apart.

"Does it matter? I'm here now, just for a bit," I said. He looked like us. A little more of Eliza's coloring, a little more of

my face, but was a perfect mix of us. He was well-fed, strong, and clean. This world couldn't have been too bad to him.

"Are you a ghost?"

"Does it matter?" I asked again.

He stopped at this and sat on his bed. A real mattress, soft, warm. "Guess not."

"How many times have you asked for this? How many times have you sat right there, with your head in your hands, and asked for just one more chance to say something to me?" It was the training. I kept telling myself that. It was the training.

"I dunno. Too many times," he said and then was quiet. I just stood there, trying not to startle him. "I'm sorry, Dad. I'm sorry."

"For what?"

"I'm sorry I stopped talking to you after you left." He began to cry. He cried like Eliza, the tears a steady trickle down, but the face never changed. "I shouldn't have been so mad."

"You can't help how you feel. I'd be mad too, I think."

"You were doing what you thought was right. You were trying to do what was best for us," he continued. "I know you were proud of your job. I know you were proud to serve. I didn't see it. I don't think I ever will."

"Maybe it was my job to make sure you didn't need to do what I did."

"I guess. I just, I hope you didn't die thinking I didn't love you." He began to cry hard at this, more of my crying, heavy sobs that shake from shoulder to hip. "I just wish I had my dad in my life, even if just a voice somewhere."

"I'm always in your life, and you're always in mine," I said. I gripped hard on my belt, so hard I remember the indentations stayed on my hands for hours.

"I'm sorry. I was angry and stupid and weak. You always told me to not be weak, to be strong for you and Mom."

"Weak and strong aren't traits, son. They are choices. Just choices. You can choose to be strong, right now. You can choose to remember that we make mistakes, we aren't perfect, but we can try to be better."

"I always thought maybe you left because you caught me with Andy, and you couldn't stand the sight of a sly boy," he said. He straightened slightly at this. It took me a minute to figure the slang out. I smiled at him. I'd seen so many worlds, something like that seemed so trivial. Most things should be trivial next to a parent's love.

"I love my son. You don't have to do or be anything but my son for me to love you. I don't care about anything else."

"Can you stay? Can you stay longer?" he asked.

I knew the answer I wanted to give.

"No. I need to go. I need you to do me a favor though." He looked at me with those dark brown eyes, and I felt half of me melt away. "Lay back. Close your eyes, and tell me about your favorite day where it was just the two of us."

"We were at the park, the old one down by the fairgrounds in our first place, the apartment," he began. My hand instinctively moved to my knife. "I was six, maybe? Some older kids were playing football, and I wanted to play, but they didn't let me." I stepped closer, his eyes still closed. I could smell his breath as he spoke. I watched his chest rise and fall, just like when he was in a crib. I marveled at how strong he had become. I marveled at what I never got to have. I had the knife ready. Training. "And you went up to them, took one of their extra balls, dared them to try and stop you, and walked back to me, and we kicked that thing for what seemed like hours, and when

*we were done, you had me bring it back to them and say thank
you. We ate iced milk after, and you told me..."*

*Training is what training is. Strength and weakness are
choices. The kid never felt the sleeping mist, probably didn't
even notice. I wanted him to feel only my lips against his
forehead. His words trailed off as the sleeping chemical hit his
nose, odorless and harmless.*

*I walked out of the room, out of that place, and went back on
my mission. It was a dead end, so I needed to find a hardened
target and start cracking.*

*I didn't make much on that Jump, but I didn't care. I got
what I needed, tucked away in my suit.*

*That wasn't real. I never got it to be real. That photo is just
a physical manifestation of delusion, and you know it.*

Nathan walked out of that place, away from the photo
of a child raised well. The data-worms did everything, and
after three days, they found no hard evidence of the theorem, even when he had managed his way into nation-state
building with robust security. The only mention of it was
on various online sites dedicated to what he deduced was an
entertainment module.

The data-worm AI was smart, but too much of what humans did, in any reality, was too specialized, too rooted in the
moment and the people, to be understood by Math. Nathan
called in that it was a dead end, the theorem was just a video
game backstory in some social platform marketing scheme.

When he left the Puddle, he saw them loading several
machines to be sent back through the Puddle. He didn't ask
any questions. He didn't care. It was harder and harder to
care.

8

Nathan had not killed himself in many years, but it was inevitable that he would again. Everything seemed inevitable. Another off-shoot was found, one with both the tech and the resources to make an honest go at Puddles. They were in the process of building them, the world split between four super-states. Each one was building, slowly. The recon drones had searched through the digital history of the world and found that one state was close. It was an arms race, the only one that mattered. Nathan had to steal what they had, mainly a plasma technology that would replace most mounted weaponry. Once Nathan was done, the atmo-killers would be launched.

Nathan had discovered them, not that he knew at the time, but they were a new type of thermonuclear weapon. They burned so hot and for so long, they lit any oxygen, hydrogen, and nitrogen atmosphere on fire. It was a clean, quick way to ensure that any Earth was no longer a threat. Even if people were underground, there was no longer any oxygen to breathe. Nathan watched them load one up as he left, ready for him to come back or to hit the fail-safe. They had custom launchers that could be propelled through the Puddle and then activated once clear.

Nathan tracked down his alternate self, and he began his usual work. He could no longer pass for himself superficially, but he could still pass any biometric security. Really, he would not need to since the data-worms found no evidence that his alternate self was involved in any usable industry, but he was expected to follow protocol. He was expected to make sure.

It was a large place by most standards, several bedrooms, a few bathrooms. It did not have a yard as the world was too dry for such, and he could see the marks from a recent dust storm. The HUD warned that the air carried numerous carcinogenic agents, and the temperature outside would be hazardous during physical exertion. There was a simple fingerprint keypad, which opened with the touch of Nathan's finger. A rush of cool, filtered air hit him, and he walked inside.

He smelled her before he heard her. Even now, decades gone, he knew what his mother smelled like. He could not remember her voice just as it was. He could not remember the touch of her hands on his head. But he could remember her smell. He carefully walked inside, watched the lives of another version of himself play out on the walls. Pictures of him as a child, living in a car rather than a shack. Nathan smiled at this. His mother must have had a good stroke of luck, got them up in the world, living in a car and working rather than scrapping.

There were pictures of a fighting ring, gloves raised in victory. Pictures of Nathan in the service, chafing under the dress uniform and the weight it carried. Pictures of him at school, grinning proudly. Pictures of him with another man, arm in arm, smiling. Pictures of a wedding, two noble figures cut against a courthouse background. A memorial picture, Nathan knew the type.

Elegant, understated, but serious. Nothing else in it but the face of someone gone, hung in the center, yet a halo of empty space around it, ostracized for the grief it carried. The other man was dead, not too long ago.

All the while, Nathan's mother was there, smiling at the camera in most of the pictures. No memorial picture of her. Nathan walked the house quietly, following the scent. He found her in a room, listening to music that was eerily familiar but mathematically improbable to be identical, sitting in a mechanized chair, staring at a vid-screen that displayed a vibrant ocean. She was old, so much older than he could have ever imagined. Her proud features buried in wrinkles, her eyes dulled by medication, her hands a knot of arthritis. Her skin looked paper thin, and her hair lost all of its kink and volume.

She was beautiful, sitting there. She was beautiful because she was there. Nathan stepped inside the room, slowly closing the door.

"Mama? How are you feelin today?" Nathan asked. She sat in her chair, her eyes unfocused, milky. She smelled like sterile ointments and her head drooped under the weight of something chemical. "Mama, you awake?"

"Nathaniel? Is that you?" she asked, a voice rough with time and decay. She reached out, and Nathan took her hand in his.

"It's me, Mama."

"You haven't called me that in years, since you went off to school," she said. Her fingers gripped the slightest bit harder.

"You feeling ok?" Nathan asked. He sat down next to her, still holding her hand.

"Tired. Always tired. I think it's all the washing. So much washing for just one little boy, " she said. Nathan looked over the room and saw nothing like laundry. "To-day, I went to work and that Mr. Johnson was there. Always so crass."

"Really? What'd you do?" Nathan asked. He had seen more than a few of the oldest residents of Bootown like this. They didn't last long.

"Oh, what I usually do. Smile and nod. Not be alone with him. Can't lose the job," she mumbled and trailed off. Nathan held her hand for a few more minutes.

"Mama, tell me a story," Nathan said, fighting the tears from his voice.

"Tired now. Go to sleep. You don't need no story tonight, " she said. Nathan had heard this, many times. "Love you, Baby Duck."

"Love you, Mama Duck," Nathan said. He kissed her gently on the forehead, and put the music machine up high. He closed the door and went back to work.

He searched the home, but there was nothing of value. This Nathan was a scholar of some kind, a doctor. His old military medals and gear tucked away in a large chest, moth-eaten and threadbare. Pictures of a marriage that ended in death rather than the defeats of life. Nathan heard the door unlock, open, and the sound of footsteps.

Old Nathan walked in. Nathan heard him go immediately to Old Mama's room. He could hear him talk with her, check her medication, and then help her into the bathroom. Once that was done, he put her back in the chair and back at the vid-screen. He walked into the kitchen, made himself a drink, and disappeared into another room. Nathan watched from a distance, trying to get the measure of the man. He

moved slow with age, a bad knee, but he walked confi-
dently. He may have been a scholar, but he still walked
like a fighter.

Old Nathan returned to the kitchen with the drink
empty and the clothes loose-fitting. He turned on music
of his own, heavy on the drum and strings, something
Nathan enjoyed, and he began to prepare a meal. Nathan
focused on his blade, pushed away the thought of Old
Mama, what would happen to her without Old Nathan
here. It did not matter. She was overdue anyway. Nathan
moved forward, blade ready, mind focused.

*I never got to see her grow old, truly old. How strange it
is that old is relative. She was always ancient to me.*

*I found her once, younger. It couldn't have been more
than a few years after she passed. It was a world like
ours, but not. The planet was still dying, but slower. The
world was still rotten, just not so much. Bootown felt like
a real city, still slowly decaying, but intact. Mama looked
younger than she could have been, but living seemed easier.*

*I watched her, watched her through a window as she
danced with a man that I had never met. I don't know if
it was my father, probably not.*

*My team was scouting, still together, mostly. We had lost
Tamayo on the last trip. Lost to somewhere. She just never
came back, never made the last opening. We didn't ask too
many questions. That Earth was simple, quiet. Not a lot of
people, not a lot of cities, just green grass, blue sky, and soft
sun. It was a nice place.*

*Elahi and I were trying to get the translator as much
data as possible. We still had Peterson, and we had some
new kid. I don't remember his name. He and Peterson were
off in another part of the city.*

"Funny how I always seem to end up here," I said, under my breath, but Elahi could hear just about anything. She always said a Farmie had to hear better than smell if they wanted to survive.

"What you see?" Elahi asked, carefully scanning a pulp mass-media text. The translators were working overtime now.

"My Mother, I think."

"Stupid luck, man. Think you exist here?"

"I don't know."

"That'd be weird," Elahi said. This was before everything. This was before we knew how to find ourselves, or at least get as close as we could manage. Within the infinite, close is a relative term. This was the first time I really knew, really saw, that something could be different.

"Yeah, weird."

"We should totally go say hi." Elahi grinned. I stepped back for a moment at the thought of it.

"You're out of your Farmie mind. How could that go well?"

"We are out here gathering data. Maybe she has a console."

"Are the verbal translators working yet?"

"Just about. Won't be pretty, but it'll work."

"Nah, seems like a big risk for little gain. Too weird," I said.

With that, Elahi sprinted into the building, shouting out my last name. I managed to catch her about half way up a flight of stairs, and there she was, peeking down the stairwell at the commotion. Mama, still somehow young in this world, much younger than ours ever allowed her to be.

"Sorry, Ma'am. She's a bit twitched," I said. Young Mama tilted her head at me.

"Well, no one needs to be shouting my daddy's name all over here. Take her somewhere else," Young Mama said with just as firm a voice as ever. Vibrant. Musical.

"You got any kids, lady?" Elahi asked as I pulled her back down the stairs.

"Not that it is any of your business, but yes. Three beautiful girls, all better behaved than you," Young Mama said. My chest tightened. I never thought of a sibling. I never stopped to think that maybe Mama was happy with some other collection of DNA. I never stopped to think that maybe Mama had a better Baby Duck.

"What is wrong with you?" I asked Elahi as we left and went to find Peterson and the kid.

"Just havin fun. This is supposed to be fun."

"This is supposed to be our job, and ain't nobody paying you for fun," I responded. Mama said that to me all the time.

"Whichever. I am going to see if my mother is here. Going to scare her something good if we get the time." Elahi laughed.

We did find consoles, and we did find Elahi. In that world, Elahi was there, actually her. She was still a Farmie, but she owned her own little slice of land to the south.

"Oh, she's apparently into XY and has three little bits. Imagine that, I like XY here and I have kids. How insane is that?" Elahi laughed. She chattered all about it, even to Peterson. He changed the conversation.

"Once we get transport, we will go down in that direction and follow protocol," Peterson said.

"Protocol? There a pre-planned prank already?" Elahi laughed. The kid looked at us both nervously.

"If there is a positive ID of an alternate team member, then the alternate must be eliminated in order to preserve mission integrity," Peterson said as flat as he could manage.

"What does it matter that there is some poor Farmie out here? How's that impact anything?" I asked. "Why we gotta do that?"

"This world has video surveillance and mass nation surveillance including digital social data-mining. If they can positively identify that there was another version of a person not from their world, it could raise suspicion and make this destination untenable for any further development."

"What are you smothering on about?" Elahi was starting to get red.

"Protocol dictates it. No discussion. Olamina can do it if that makes you more comfortable."

"I ain't doing nothing," I said. The Company could never make me kill for them, not like this. I used to believe that.

"Protocol dictates it."

"Who cares? It don't matter, so don't make it matter," Elahi said, her hand dropping to her blade out of instinct.

"It matters because it is protocol, you stupid Farm-Kite," Peterson finally exploded. He jabbed his finger right between Elahi's eyes, and for the first time, he looked like he was trying to be the big rat that the world always told him he was. "There is no more discussion. You will burn that whole place to the ground with everyone in it if I tell you to do it because I am..." Peterson couldn't finish the thought before Elahi took his throat with her blade.

The kid had some instinct to him, and he had drawn his own blade and brought it all the way up Elahi's back. Unfortunately for him, he didn't have the instinct to defend himself, only his Commander. Elahi managed to twist the blade into him as she went down. She was the toughest of us; the kid just didn't know that.

"Had, had to protect my babies," Elahi half laughed, half sputtered. "That's what Mothers do, right?" She sputtered again, fighting her dying nerves, fighting to keep breathing. I held her hand, and told her about all the food that we'd eat

when she was stitched up. When she died, died laughing to a joke only she understood: "They can never change me now." my HUD unlocked the command feature, and suddenly, I was in charge of no one. Protocol dictated I burn the bodies with the special gel Peterson had hidden on him.

"Burn so bright that dust can't hide you." Our goodbye.

I have watched my friends and family die for this. I have watched everything be taken from me for this. Just do it again.

Nathan brought himself back with the blade, finding its purpose, his purpose. Old Nathan noticed the danger, some part of him smelled the change in the air, felt that sensation when another means you harm. He had lived a hard life. A life constantly looking over his shoulder because he refused to hide or he could not hide. Old Nathan reacted out of trained instinct. He had yet to truly see his opponent, see the mirror waiting to be shattered. He simply lashed out with the cooking knife in his hand, catching Nathan off guard and taking a piece of his lip with it.

The two fought, and while Nathan was stronger, he was not superior, simply better. Nathan's blade found flesh several times, several kill shots, but none clean. Old Nathan managed a kitchen knife into the lower back, snipping nerve and damaging bone. Old Nathan knew he was dead, but he took his attacker's blade in the promise of a mortal wound in return. Both fell. Both stared.

Nathan focused on his training. He took out the nanofoam hidden in his belt and sprayed it into the wound. It would take an hour, maybe less, for him to walk again, but he would not bleed out. Old Nathan was bleeding inside the half-cauterized wound, his stomach and lungs slowly filling, his blood slowly poisoned. They stared at each other, both the same age, one looking like a bad memory of youth, the other like a terrible warning of age.

9

"This is awkward," Nathan finally said, more to himself. Old Nathan just stared. "It's nothing personal."

"What are you?" Old Nathan said, fighting to form the words.

Nathan had a moment of indecision. It didn't matter though, not at the end. Nathan told him everything. Everything. Perhaps it was death creeping, but Old Nathan accepted the premises rather easily, considering it all. He took it in, studied it, and found no reason to doubt, not given the fact that he was staring at himself, more or less, 40 years younger with a glowing blade and neuro-tech.

"So that's the long and short of it," Nathan finished.

"You've killed entire populations?"

"Me? Just once. My people? I don't know. Above my pay grade."

"So I'm a monster in another world. Another life, I could have been a monster."

"Not particularly. What I do isn't monstrous, no more than the Farmie is monstrous to the crop."

"People aren't plants." Old Nathan spat violently. A surge of hatred pushed him forward, but his body was spent. His mind could only rage, trapped inside a soon to be inactive shell.

"I think you know that's not true," Nathan said. He looked around the modest but cherished home. "What percentage of your planet lives in poverty? What percentage lives and dies in filth, in ignorance, in violence?"

"A lot," Old Nathan responded in shame. He saw no reason to lie either. Minutes passed as the men stared at each other, unsure of how to proceed.

"Do you have a family?" Old Nathan asked.

"Used to, long time ago."

"What happened?"

"The world was garbage."

"What happened?" Old Nathan pushed.

"Stupid luck," Nathan said as cold as he felt. "You seem like you had it nice."

"We always wanted to adopt, but they wouldn't let us. You ever been to a place where people didn't care about that?"

"More than a few."

"Dumb luck, then," Old Nathan said.

"Stupid luck." Nathan looked over the dying man and back to the rest of the house. "You still had it nicer than just about everyone where I'm from, so count your blessings."

"So every world is sick, just like this one."

"It was like that for us, once. If you weren't born into a place where a random act of violence, disease, or starvation killed you, you were damn, damn lucky. Hell, even if you were born to a decent place, chances are, you broke your own mind trying to keep it. Hard to care about what somebody else is doing when you can barely eat enough to live."

"Doesn't justify anything," Old Nathan said while coughing up red.

"It sure does. I can smell the dust here. I can see the blurry horizon. This planet is dying to fuel what you think is advancement. Back home, the skies are blue, the water is clean, and the air doesn't poison you, all because we found an Earth with eco-restoration technology."

"So why not share it with us?"

"Cause you're a threat. Every world that figures out how to Jump is a threat to ours, and I ain't gonna have that."

"So you'll just kill a few of us and let the rest of us die."

"Let's be real: reality is zero-sum. Somebody has to lose, but if you can jump worlds, you can make a few people in a few worlds lose so everyone in another world wins." Nathan felt small twinges in his legs as the nano-machines began to reconnect the nerves in his spine. "Can't have competition for that."

"Why do you get to decide that?"

"Because we figured out how first. Basic evolution. We adapted first, so we thrive first."

"And what if God thinks differently?"

"I've been to so many worlds with so many Gods, I'm not sure any of them are keeping track," Nathan said. "Seriously, you name a deity on your rock, and chances are they are nonexistent somewhere else. That sound like we've figured out this whole God thing?"

"There's a God. Just because we don't know the name, doesn't mean it's not there," Old Nathan said. He clutched a small metal trinket on his neck.

"If that makes you feel better." Nathan almost laughed. "I've killed a planet, Took. Don't you think that planet's God would've stopped me?"

"What happens when you run out of worlds to pillage? Does your world stay a dream?" Old Nathan asked.

Nathan knew this was a concern. Peak-Reality. At some theoretical point, his world would be the most advanced in existence, save for the ever branching pathways of causality. At some point, the only worlds left to exploit would be subtle variations of his own, and the wars would ravage it all. Eventually, some mirror of his world would decide to purge it all in an ever-constant state of trans-dimensional warfare. This logically only ensured that his world must eradicate every other.

"We have contingencies for that," Nathan said flatly. He was one of them.

"Contingencies. You sound like a corporate man if I ever heard one."

"What do you know about it? How'd you get this shiny life, huh?"

"That woman in there worked her hands to the bone to send me to school. To raise me out of a city where everyone wanted to shit on me and call it a favor. I didn't come from anywhere fancy, but I made this life."

"She sure didn't teach you manners," Nathan said. "So this nation-state? How rich is it compared to the rest of the world?" Nathan asked. "Cause I am willing to bet that if you were raised in a shantytown, pulling copper pipes outta buildings all day while trying not to sell yourself for quick credits, you probably wouldn't have this."

"I worked for this."

"And the game was already rigged. Cause there are a billion other poor kids that ain't never gonna have a chance because they weren't born in the right place or the right time. You won a minimum prize: a not miserable life. You were never gonna get more than that."

"Everyone has to build their own life. We aren't slaves to chance."

"Sure we are. It was chance that I'm here, of all places. It was chance that I was born to the Earth that was going to create trans-dimensional travel. It was chance that you didn't turn around a second earlier and bury that knife in my throat,"Nathan said, his voice rising. "Chance is all there is. If you want a God, there it is. Luck. Pretend all you want to the contrary, but I am the one walking out of here and taking whatever your Earth can give me to make mine better."

"What gives you the right to judge me? To judge us? You're just a hired murderer, a thief," Old Nathan said, his eyes starting to flicker in some last moment of defiance.

"I ain't judging. I'm harvesting. I'm building a life for all of my people, not just some."

"You're destroying a life right now."

"If it helps serve billions of people? You're goddamn right I am." Nathan tried to make his legs work. The nanofoam was not quite finished connecting the nerves back. "This ain't about team, or tribe, or country, or Corp, or race, or religion. I built a life for my world. All of them. Can you say that?"

"The world isn't my responsibility," Old Nathan muttered.

"Now who's selfish? Now who is the monster? You'd let some little boy's mama die of a curable disease because you don't want to get your hands dirty?"

"You don't have the right."

"There are no rights. There is a damn near infinite number of you. Hell, right now, across who knows how many realities, we've done so much worse and loved it."

"Not me."

"Really? What do you think makes us different?"

"I hated having to hurt people, no matter the reason. People deserve better than pain."

"You don't get it. I don't care if you're real or not. I don't care if my God is the true god or not. I don't care because none of that matters to me. All that matters is that I get what I need from this place. And if I have to murder a collection of atoms that happen to resemble my Mama, who died painfully for me some forty years ago, then sure. Why not?" Nathan was almost shouting at this point, pushing himself up with his arms and balancing against the counter.

"You are sick. A genocidal maniac with delusions. Right now, you could choose to be the one that saves billions of people"

" I am saving billions!"

"You know what you are."

"No, I make sure that kids don't die of leukemia, that garbage turns into food, that eight billion people have a future."

"At what cost?"

"At any," Nathan growled. He felt a hatred rise up in him like never before. "So what's your life been like, huh? Why is your life so damned important that you'd deny a million children a better life? That you'd accept your own child dying because he was born five years too early to be saved!" Nathan screamed, his face red from the exertion of trying to stand under his own power. "Did you have to watch your baby boy die because he was born five years too early to be saved by a goddamn injection?! Wouldn't you murder universe after universe to make sure that never happens again? Isn't anything worth that?"

"You had a son?" Old Nathan asked after a few quiet moments. His voice was fading, but it was soft, almost kind. "What was his name?" Nathan sat for more quiet moments. He did not want to say, but he did not want to lie. He remembered Marissa's words in her letter: *You can lie to me, to the world, but don't lie to yourself.*

"Luis, after Mama," Nathan said. "He was beautiful, more than even her."

"What was it like, being a dad?" Old Nathan spoke again. "All my life, I just wanted something like that."

"It was being human in a way you never knew you could be," Nathan said, tears trickling down his cheeks. "It was being so happy, so scared, so tired, so sorry for what you couldn't give and so thankful for what you had. It was the best and worst thing ever to happen to me, in every place I've ever been." Nathan's tears stopped. He pushed his body to work, but the nerves weren't there yet. He gripped his knife and felt its reality. "And then it was taken from me, and I've spared billions of parents that pain since. You'd do the same if my life was yours."

"'My life.' Don't you hear how selfish you sound? You've killed dozens of worlds in order to save your own! You could have saved a hundred billion little ones, but you don't because someone convinced you that the work is righteous."

"This whole place is going to be ash in a few days anyway, so it don't matter a thing what you think," Nathan said, relying on his returning anger to fuel him forward.

"You think she would be proud of you? You think your son would be proud of you?" Old Nathan coughed out as his body shut down.

Nathan could not stop the tears now, his face wet and his body shaking.

"You could have chosen differently. You could have been better than this, maybe somewhere, you are."

Despite that the nanofoam hadn't come close to finishing, Nathan limped as best he could, and he buried the blade into Old Nathan's throat.

It was over.

"God damnit, I am proud of my fuckin self." Nathan said to anyone listening.

No one was.

COMMUTER

Going to Work

The Out The Door Checklist mattered: Keys. Cell. Multi-tool. Nicotine gum. Combat knife. Sidearm. Four extra mags: two standard, one hollow, one armor piercing. Time to go shopping.

My Nana likes to tell stories about how shopping was something different. Then one day monsters were real. A lot of people died. We figured it out. And now here I am, making sure that I rack the slide on my dad's old Glock, even though he'd yell at me, if he was still alive.

Will taught me this. He didn't mean to, but he didn't mean for any of it to happen either. We were running an old job, Sparrow Collections, which means driving around town, picking up personal electric scooters from low-traffic areas and depositing them back in high traffic areas. On the surface, it was an easy gig, and the company even sprang for gas, but being on the road that much, especially in the boondocks, was not particularly quick money.

Inside the main heart of the city, things are generally copesetic. BDE squads are out in force, particularly in the business areas. The actual municipal police still patrolled the most trafficked areas, so there was another layer of redundancy if anything went sideways. Being downtown or at the higher end shopping zones, life was pretty stress free in terms of not being randomly killed by some genetic abomination, and that was where 90% of Sparrows were used and available.

The problem is you get kids—mostly kids as they were the only ones dumb enough to try and take an electric scooter to the boonies—who went from a shopping zone to a domestic block. This was usually on a dare, or they found a way to hack the tracking on the Sparrow to let them ride for free or dirt cheap. Buses and subways are major targets for BDs, so I can't blame them for trying to get home safely and cheaply, two things that are usually mutually exclusive. So you get a Sparrow stuck in some housing zone, and well, unless it was a nice one that could afford constant patrols, they were always miserable with BDs.

Finding the Sparrow was always easy; they had GPS locators, so you knew where they were down to six inches, and you generally had a nice Sat-image to show you what was around it as of 5 minutes ago. The problem was of course leaving the safety of the vehicle and putting the damn thing into the trunk or backseat. You split the pay fifty-fifty if you had a partner, and a partner was essential: one on gun, one on scooter.

Will showed me the ropes. We were friends in high school, and we both dreamed the same dreams about college until the rent came due and we had to wake up. We figured we could make good scratch doing Sparrow and we had each other's backs, just like at school. We went to a shitty public one with three resource officers for three acres and five thousand students, and the ROs cared more about putting kids in prison rather than taking down BDs, so you figure you'd lose a kid or two a week.

Will was my lockdown buddy, and so I trusted him. We once dodged a HellCat together, Will taking a piece of its eye with a pair of scissors before we managed to get into the closet and lock it shut. He was a good guy, just enough crazy-cool to make life enjoyable but never so much of a troll that he liked to watch others take it.

We'd take turns between gun and scooter, and at our best, we could retrieve a scooter in seven seconds from doors opening to car moving again. When you're that fast, most BDs didn't even have the chance to register you. That is, until there was a problem.

"Fuck, it's stuck in the fucking bush!" I yelled, yanking on the scooter. Whoever last used it had the goddamn audacity to tie it to the bush. Maybe they planned on using it again.

"Use your knife!" Will returned. His voice faded for a second, his head scanning wildly. I drew my knife and started on the cord. "Incoming!" Will screamed, raising the rifle to his shoulder. It was a HellCat of course. They were once Mountain Lions, I think, but HellCats were pure black, a black so rich that it swallowed light. Even in the daytime, it was almost impossible to see them unless they were against a bright surface. Their teeth could bite through a steel pole, and their claws were five inches of Kevlar shredding bullshit. They could sprint like a goddamn Cheetah, and I've seen one jump a good twenty feet in a single bound.

The Hellcat was on Will. Maybe it smelled the fear. Maybe he was a millimeter closer. Maybe it was just bad luck. But the HellCat went right for him. Will had his gun shouldered, and he pressed the trigger with a single, clean motion, and the last thing he heard before his own screaming was the click of a firing pin hitting nothing. There was no round chambered. Then the Hellcat hit him, one claw across the face, and instantly, that not-quite-good-looking but certainly not ugly face was in distinct pieces. Will screamed and dropped the rifle.

I drew my sidearm and unloaded. Hellcats were at least easy to put down, if you got the shot. The problem was Will. He was on the ground, bleeding out. There was nothing I could do, and even if a full ER team was there with the whole set up, he'd still have died. All I could do was load his body into his own truck, right next to the scooter. The next prick who wanted to rent the ones we found would have to wipe the blood off first.

His parents, now childless, let me keep the truck. I couldn't. I sold it, but it was the down payment on Deductible. That's about as good as it gets, sometimes.

Sometimes, I hear Dad's voice in my head about keeping a round chambered, how that was stupid, an easy way to negligent discharge yourself into the next life, if such a thing existed, but he didn't have to watch Will scream until there was too much blood. Better be ready. Life was different for Dad. He was too used to the old world, the way things were when he was a kid.

He died to some BD, not sure what. They never found it, and most of them slash you up good, so it could have been anything. He went out for a run at night, trying to lose the gut that he blamed on his job and his family.

"Just the media trying to get their advertising dollars," he said before he left. Mom and I both warned him. "Still more likely to die from Heart Disease." He gave his odd half-laugh, half-snort when he felt self-assured.

"Love, maybe just wait until the morning and go to the gym?" Mom asked in that way that wasn't asking but recommending the wiser course of action.

"Too much to do in the morning, and after ten years of this one always waking up before five am..." he pointed at me with a smile. I had been a terrible sleeper until puberty started to give me all sorts of other problems. "I like sleeping in as much as I can."

With that, he went out for a quick run. He never came back. At least we got to bury him. When the BDs went full crazy in the first Migration, most people were buried in a mass grave. He was an early one.

Mom and I spent the next six weeks locked in our home, sirens a constant, our grief this slow fog that muddled every-thing, and sometimes, when you weren't looking, it filled the room until you were alone. We lost the house afterwards. That's when we moved in with Nana in her place out in the boonies, the mortgage paid off a few years earlier. Not that we could keep that house for long. But we made the right choice to move closer to the city.

These thoughts are not part of the checklist. Sometimes, I have to remind myself that "Stay Present" is always the last box at the end of any list. There is work to do. The hustle only knows forward. I have to go shopping.

Well, shopping for other people. I tend to think of myself as a professional traveler. That's the best way to singularly encompass my earnings. I have several jobs, and all of them involve traveling. They have other similarities as well that I ponder, walking the subway cars, trying to keep some sense of awareness while also entertaining myself. The boredom is real, no matter what.

"Everything becomes old hat," Nana would say to me. She was born before a cell phone, born before people just rented cars every day. More importantly, she remembers life before things like Raptors, Arnies, and every other action franchise that's become part of the real world because some scientists have no imagination, only imitation. She has lived longer in the world before than ours now, but to her credit, she's adapted really fucking well.

We live together. When courting a fine young caller, I will say that she lives with me, but really, we live together. She pays rent just like I do, and she covers the net while I cover electricity. We each take care of our own cell plans because we both have too good of plans to ever change, plans from back in the day. They were both originally family plans, but we are the only family left to each other. Our data needs are generally more than what a personal plan allocates. Rationing is real, even when it comes to data.

She needs it. She runs two different call centers from our apartment, and managing over twenty-thousand AI customer service reps isn't easy. We are lucky she has the job. Working from home? Pretty sweet. Granted, the companies are supposed to pay her back for the data usage, but well, there's always something.

"One day, they'll run out of excuses and fake charges, at least for a month or so, and then we get a bigger place," Nana says as I head out the door.

"Why? I like this place," I reply, like always. "Good steel door, ten floors up, all reinforced glass around that's impossible to climb."

She smiles and nods. "We do sleep good, don't we?"

"We sure do," I say as I walk out the door.

Maybe she is right. It'd be nice to have a home, a real one. Saladin—one of my usual partners when I'm doing the BDE rounds—he always tells me to save up to buy a house.

"That's where the real wealth begins. Allah ain't making any more land," he has said to me more times than I can count. "A lab can make just about any creature out of spare DNA and stem cells, but nobody has figured out how to make new, livable land."

"Not yet. It's probably in development." At this point, I assume just about everything is in development, somewhere. Thing is, he spends almost all his cash on fortifying and repairing his place, and then the HOA fees are fucking theft. My GroceryGopher job would only cover half of what he pays for the complex security's monthly fee. I'd rather live two hundred feet in the air with floors of other targets below me.

I don't say that. It would be rude.

I do own my own car, which is a bit of a splurge, but luckily, it is tax deductible. Being born to a set of accountant parents sounds dull as shit, and all the old sitcoms made it seem like the worst possible punishment for a young, rowdy fool, but you know, knowing the loopholes in the tax system is really cool. Nana and I would be packed into some low-rent, low-security feeder box, just waiting for some bullshit to eat us or get trampled to death if we didn't know how to maximize our deductions. I mean, it is a hassle to have to count shells and then write up the paperwork to show that they were discharged for business purposes, but hey, every little bit counts.

Saladin never chastises me about the truck. It makes our life easier. Since we both work BDE and GroceryGopher, it helps to split gas when we travel. I even gave him the digital forms so he could deduct the gas money that he gives me. As most people who use GroceryGropher tend to live in the same areas, we can do multiple trips in one car ride, and having a large, armored truck bed means we can carry a lot of groceries. Saladin likes to call the car "Amu," which

I can't remember if that is some Somali folklore reference or a comic book character. Doesn't matter. I call my truck "Deductible" because fuck yeah, everything about it is.

Also, because it is mine, I get to write things on it. When I open the recessed trunk in the bed, spray painted in black is the Commute Checklist: Armor. Secure Rifle. Secure Shotty. Check First Aid. Check Cigarettes. Check Gas.

Every morning thus begins the process. I keep the heavy gear in the trunk because honestly, it scares Nana. I think she forgets what I do, and she grew up in rural Texas, so the idea of someone putting a pistol on their hip was always old hat for her. Full body armor, including shin and forearm guards, a chainmail scarf to protect the neck, and a combat helmet? Yeah, that is not normal to her.

Part of me thinks it would be smarter to armor up in the apartment where it is safer, but our garage has solid security, and my parking space is right in front of one of the guard stations with the .50 calibur, so I don't worry too much. In the morning, it is usually Levi manning it, just like today. He waves from behind a solid foot of bullet proof glass, the glare of all his cameras and sensors bouncing off his pale face. He lives in the building, as the landlord's son this is his only job. He's told me that he streams his juggling and dexterity tricks every night, but I doubt that keeps a roof over his head. Still, he's reliable. Once, when one of those damn super irritated Wasps got in, big as my truck and pissed off, the .50 cal didn't hesitate, and well, a giant Wasp is scary and shit, but the Russians, the Chinese, the Iranians, or whoever the fuckever the media likes to blame for all this, they can't seem to build anything with solid steel for skin, yet. In development, I'm sure.

I know exactly how much of a bitch the clean up on that thing is, but that's what JiffyCleans are for. That was one of my first jobs, but after you cleaned up literally twenty pounds of genetically augmented intestines, the glamor wears off the whole ordeal. Once, two different Arnies got loose into a low-rent housing block. Just one seven foot, quasi-humanoid with knives for fingers and bone density five times higher than a human can do some real fucking damage, especially since they are built out of chimpanzee DNA, so they don't kill to eat you like other BDs. No, these fuckers just enjoy killing. Two of them hit the same block, one from the top, one from the bottom. Those poor bastards, over eighty of them dead in just a few minutes. Carnage so bad, it actually made the news.

That's what I remember; that's what I remind myself every day I feel like complaining about any of my gigs. I remember picking up a bloodied rag that once was a little girl and placing her inside a small, black temporary coffin. I remember bleaching out the blood from where she died. I remember scraping tufts of her hair caked against the wall. I remember the silence of the housing block. A few hundred people living side by side, all of them shuffling around us as we cleaned, no room to go anywhere and too damn scared to go outside. After that, I stopped JiffyCleans. The pay was shit too, I guess.

I check each gun's chamber, ensuring there is something waiting for me. I make sure the safety is on. I place the rifle and the shotgun in their racks behind the driver's seat. I make sure the extra magazines are where they should be in the center console, right next to the cigarettes. It is a lot of double checking. That is the nature of life, the nature of the grind. You have to make sure, or rather, ensure that you have done all that you can do to set yourself up for success. After that, the dice just roll, and whether you come home with fat tips or don't come home at all, that's out of your hands. But from my experience, taking the time to set yourself up is what makes sure that the dice don't fuck you.

GroceryGropher

The Morning Commute checklist: Pick up Saladin on Mondays, Wednesdays, Fridays, Saturdays. Pick up Rita on Tuesdays, Thursdays, and Saturdays. Get gas. Start the App. Plot course. Make money.

It is a Saturday, which is good since it's a big money day. I merge onto the I-5X and begin the trek to get Saladin and Rita. They live on separate sides of the city, but they take turns commuting over to the other's place to save us all time and a bit of gas money. Rita is usually quick on the spot with the app and getting our orders lined up, so sometimes we audible as Rita meeting us at store might save more time, which means more cash. Today, no such luck, but Rita already braved the Metro and as far as I know, is safe at Saladin's, probably helping him repair something for a bit of extra change.

Saladin doesn't live too far into the boonies, and it is at least a nicer one. His community has a twenty-foot wall lined with razor-wire and every square inch is surveyed by both standard cameras and a few IR drones. There is a proper gatehouse with 24/7 security. They all know me, know my truck, and I have all the right identification to enter without much hassle: RF chip decals of all my gigs. Between Grocery-Gopher, Ziptrip, and BDE, there is hardly a place that I can't enter, at least in civilian areas. One quick scan, and I drive up the well-manicured streets, pothole free, and stop right at Saladin's rather impressive two bedroom home, complete with crisp, green astroturf lawn.

I give them a quick pulse on their phones. They appear from the doorway, Saladin's wife always trailing behind, wishing her husband safe travels. It is sweet. It makes me smile each time. She never really acknowledges me though. Rita looks pissed today, but that happens. She's just that type of person: easy to get into a bad mood, but even in her foulest, she still managed to give you advice that, as much as you hated to admit, was often right. Saladin and Rita hustle over, the doors unlocked, and they slide into their respective positions, him up front due to his long legs, and Rita in the back where she could focus on our routes.

"Dust off now. We have four orders within half a mile of each other, can hit the MegaMatt's on Seventh," Rita barks. She used to be military, but not anymore. She hit her end of contract, and they didn't renew. I'd be salty about that too. It was steady work if you got into the permanent ranks.

"C-Von on Baseline is closer to them," Saladin says, checking his own app.

"MM is on the way, so no back tracking if we load up first and then hit the spots," Rita counters. "We can also gas up after the last drop off, so save time now." I link my truck's display to Rita's map, and we are off. We sail through the checkpoint, and at this time of morning, there isn't much traffic to get back to the interstate and closer to the city. The first part of the grocery run is quiet. We are all still in our heads, trying to map out the day and hoping the pieces land the way they need to land.

"Life is a puzzle, but the pieces just drop out of the box, and if they fit together, great. If not, well, too bad for you," Rita would say whenever we got dinged by a review for being too late or not smiling enough at the drop off. Some people even marked us down because of the combat gear and firearms, but that was only common in the city. In the boonies, people appreciated it.

We don't listen to music. We have our BD scanner on since we are all BDE, and if there's a paycheck somewhere nearby, well, better to be late for a Foodtube/GroceryGopher drop than not snagging a BD at all. We also have our BDE ping on, making sure we know where everyone else is to try and not poach anyone's payday. There are plenty of pricks who do this, slide in at the last moment, put a bullet into a corpse and demand a cut of the bounty. Our RF badges all have GPS sync as well, and the algorithm is easy to fool. Plus, it's in the company's interest to split the bounty anyway since they took a service fee out of each of us, so the more BDEs on one kill, the more they make from the government purse. It's the reason they require us to work in pairs at minimum. They tell you it's for worker safety, but they don't give much of a fuck about that.

Rita's the only one of us who could work BDE solo, only because she is military trained. She doesn't do it often though. She's smarter than that. Only when a big bill shows up out of nowhere. I worry about her that way. We're work friends, but we're still friends. Not that I have non-work friends anymore.

The scanner is dull. There is a confirmed Bugaloo sighting, but it is on the northwest end of the boonies, and there are already two teams close by. It isn't worth the drive and the low rating from our GroceryGopher. I drive on, keeping an eye on the traffic readout. Every minute matters, and if the interstate suddenly locks up or our exit is closed, that could be the difference between a good tip and no tip at all.

We make it to the MM, and thankfully, most of the traffic is other FoodTubes. All the competing apps are here, but professional shoppers are far more efficient than the few sad sacks that get their own groceries. Maybe they do it to cut costs. Maybe they are lonely. Nana said that it was easy to meet a good piece of meat at the grocery store. Her youth must have been wild.

Rita, Saladin, and I split up, each with a list. We have a clear system, one that I created of course. We each shop for the other's clients as well as our own. We all know the other's orders thanks to an app I created with Nana's help. It made sure that we could tackle the different sections of the store without having to double back or retread steps.

I hit the produce, bulk, loose food, and frozens. Saladin takes off at a near sprint to the paper goods, boxed foods, and Rita is our slippy, tackling all the random requests that don't neatly fall into the other two categories. She's the fastest and most aggressive, and she can body check just about anyone out of her way if need be. The other Foodtubers make things professionally polite. There is little browsing, little back and forth over whether the kids would want macaroni or riga-toni, so aisles move well.

A crash wakes me up out of the hunt for apples. We hadn't hit this MM before, so my eyes were on the signs hovering above the isles, not on the clock around me. A cart pushes mine off course, before another FoodTuber rushes past me to snag the dwindling sets of not-yet-ripe bananas. Fuck. I need those. My order was quite clear on "mostly green" bananas. Fucking up those kind of requests meant shitty tips. I have a feeling the kid is in the same position as me, but nah, I need to get mine.

I push my cart, letting the momentum guide it, and now I am damn near sprinting. I slide right around him, taking the force of his cart into my thigh, but I have armor there too, and it is enough to stop the cart and stop him. I use the impact to push myself forward, and with an outstretched arm, I snag the greenest bunch there is.

"Hey, fuck off, bitch!" the kid yells. There are still a few bunches left, but they are mostly yellow. He inspects me, sees the armor, sees the sidearm, and he does the calculus. He has one play left. He reaches down to his hip and fumbles for his scanner. I left mine in the cart. I didn't do the grocery checklist and failed to attach it to the rig on my plate holder.

I tuck the bananas into my body and shuffle as fast as my posture allows. I can hear the frantic clicks, even with the top pop hits of a decade ago floating through the store. I have yet to hear that sweet ting that means he has marked and paid for the bananas. He is faster than me now, but my body is shielding the barcode. He is focused on getting the shot, but like any target shooting, he needs to anticipate where I am going to be, not where I was. I stand straight up, keeping my back to him, and I reach out to get my own scanner. I hear the ting right as his hand touches my shoulder, his grip going from firm to weak. I turn and push his arm away, the bananas going into my bag, and my now free hand dropping down to my thigh.

He steps back, knowing he has lost, but that is when animals are most dangerous. Any FoodTuber will have some weapon on them for safety, whether it be Scrap-Dashers, BDs, or other Tubers. He isn't BDE, which means he has no legal right to carry a firearm in public, probably just starting out and can't afford the guard card, but that doesn't mean much. It does change the math though because it goes from an interpersonal dispute that gets out of hand to armed robbery with an unlicensed firearm, a life sentence to hard labor. The ConTeams are always hungry for meat, and he is young and strong, so they'll get a lot of value out of him.

"Fucking Fluid. Hope a BD gets you," the kid says as he turns back to his cart.

"You're not worth the seconds, man," I say as I continue to look for apples. I am relieved. Having to draw on the kid and wing him, that would cost me, Saladin, and Rita bad. The store security would have to fill out paperwork, and I'd have to give a statement, and maybe turn in the firearm until I was cleared of any likely malfeasance. In short, he's not worth my time in the real sense. I finish produce, and head to the frozen section.

The aisles are wide, easy to move between people stopping to snag their wares. There used to be more demand for frozens in general, but electricity isn't getting any cheaper, and most people ditch the freezer in general. Consumption-Mindful refrigerators. Hell, Nana and I have one. Between her systems and the usual needs, we suck up a lot of power. It only holds a few days of food but hey, it forces you to buy food that you will eat.

The list is lean, which makes sense since we are heading to the boonies. If you could afford a box full of frozen food, you could afford to live in the city. If you could afford to live in the city, you probably had a Micro in your own building, so you could shop in comfort, have leisurely conversations with neighbors over how excellent the apples are this time of year or some such bullshit. I don't know; that's what they do in the movies.

My take is mostly ice cream, the kind branded with the latest youth fad and with digital coupons for various apps. A few packs of ice cream says birthday party to me. I hope the kid gets something nice. I hope everyone follows standard protocol for large gatherings. At least a good three quarters of the BDs out there are instinctively programmed to seek out herds, so the more people in one place, the more the BDs get riled up.

The general equation was one armed guard per five people. It was also always suggested to keep at least six feet apart from other patrons so a single BD will only kill one person at a time rather than kill and injure several at once. I missed half my own Godson's christening because I was on door duty, and good thing since a Raptor and a Hellcat came calling. I mean, bonus, I actually made money on the christening, but still, it certainly changed the mood of the day.

David and his family moved away last year, far out into Alaska, far away from anywhere worth bothering. I understand that. I miss him though. He was the last reminder that I had a life before all of this.

Saladin and Rita meet me at the packaging station. We sort out our orders—my system makes this a breeze—and the machine neatly packages them all together into disposable, sterilized plastic bags, sealed for safety. I took my Nana shopping once, and all she could say was: "That was my first job, bagging groceries." I laughed at this, but she didn't. She didn't laugh much for a while after that.

We load up as fast as we can. Deductible has a full bed, and we are off. The mood is lighter now since we are in line with our estimates. Our apps have a timer feature, and while we have a rather generous delivery window, the reality is that if you didn't hit green, you weren't getting a good tip. We are still comfortably in the green, likely to arrive at the earliest end of our window.

"Traffic is clear on all main routes," Rita chimes. Her voice is a bit softer, higher than normal. She is excited.

"You about to hit the green goal for the month?" Saladin asks, a wide smile with no hint of jealousy. I am a little bit jealous.

"Assuming we land these three orders, hell yeah," Rita returns, and the two exchange forearm bumps.

"I might make it this month. Maybe," Saladin says. "A blasted Garbage Gecko almost ate through my roof last week. I could use the bonus."

"Everyone ok?" I ask. A Garbage Gecko is generally a low threat BD—a pissed off mix of a Racoon and Monitor lizard, but they have big teeth, and they carry more than just rabies. Saladin has a lot of kin living with him, which is the only way to survive. He's lucky that he got them into the country in the first place. Seems like every year, there's more and more restrictions. Must be nice to have a house so full of people you love.

"My brother-in-law took a nibble in the arm. No fever, so he should be ok," Saladin says. He smiles at me; he is always smiling, but I know his smiles. This is the *thank you for caring* one. "He can still work, so all good."

"Let's try and get you that bonus then," Rita says.

We take the off-ramp into the boonies, and we get right with ourselves. Saladin focuses on his BDE pings, looking for reports. Rita is on visual scan. Rita calls out a few Garbage Geckos, a possible Wasp, but nothing worth stopping for. All of our orders are within five blocks of each other, but this is not a self-contained drop. We are going into Sprawls, and that means no guards, no walls, just row after row of houses and lots of places to hide.

"Drop incoming," Rita says, her voice low and focused now. "Let's get paid and get home."

Saladin and I nod. Rita reaches around from the back and takes the rifle. She's always best with it, seeing as it is a civilian version of what she had for a time. Every time she holds it, there's a glimmer of memory in her eyes. It always fades into the dullness of the present.

Before Deductible can even stop, Rita and Saladin's doors are open. Saladin is the strongest, so he moves to gather the groceries. Rita is right on him, the rifle shouldered, the safety off. She is scanning. I exit with the shotgun, facing out. Rita covers Saladin and herself; I cover Deductible and Rita. Saladin's only job is to get the groceries to the door as fast as possible and with no breakage. He does carry a pistol, but it is holstered.

"Moving!" Rita says. This is my signal to shift position, closing the door and moving to cover Rita's blind spot. I keep my back to her. She keeps her back to me. We have a rhythm, a music that only we know. I move with her, and she moves with Saladin, and he moves with me.

"Clearclear Clearclear Clearclearclear," he says as we move, setting a tempo while also giving us his own scans. "Dropping!" he booms to let us know to hold in over-watch. I hear the bags hit the concrete outside the home, the door reinforced with sheet metal, the windows covered by a nest of razor wire. I hear the airy jingle of the app confirming delivery, complete with a quick snapshot. "Green!"

With that, it is my turn to lead. I move forward, retracing my steps back to the driver's side. Saladin has his pistol drawn now as he moves into the center again, watching my back while Rita watches all of our backs.

We repeat this several times, getting each of our deliveries down well within the green. The tips are decent, but nothing exceptional by any means.

The real money comes when we smell the blood.

Someone's dog was let out of the house without a minder, and maybe because it was a big as shit German Shepard, they figured it'd be fine, but they never are. Dogs are a good force multiplier, a good alarm system, but they don't handle the BDs well without help.

It was a Hellcat, and we could see the blood trail up to the tree. We found most of the dog in the bushes, Saladin calling it out as we returned to Deductible. Rita's fast on the draw, getting a bead on the thing mostly by the fact that the poor dog's collar was still in its mouth, the now dulled metal catching just a bit of light. She lets off three quick rounds, and we hear that half growl, half whine as it falls from the tree.

Saladin moves closer to take a quick snapshot on the app. It's easy money, all told, but that makes me suspicious. While Rita keeps her rifle trained on the corpse, I turn to watch our back, and there it is. Hellcats don't generally work in teams, but they do mate for life, and mates share hunting territory. The female hides under Deductible, and now I can't shoot without fucking up my ride.

"Got a situation here," I say, and both turn. "Not it."

"Not it," Rita follows.

"Shit," Saladin says. He tightens his grip on his pistol and darts to our left. The Hellcat immediately follows, moving fast from under the truck to intercept him. I shoot first, aiming for its back legs. The buckshot rips one hind leg off and sends the creature tumbling. Saladin trips. The HellCat is too close to him for Rita to shoot. Pistol at the ready, he fires a clean shot to the head. We all scan again. Saladin laughs as he takes another snapshot, and then we all pile back into Deductible as fast as we can.

"Two for one, not bad," Rita says. Saladin is out of breath, laughing to calm his nerves. Our apps all ring at once.

"They are paying less and less for Hellcats," I say.

"Well, they just aren't as hot as they used to be I guess," Rita responds. Our various grocery apps ding again, and we have new orders. The morning continues until we have to get our swole on. Or rather, get paid for others to get their swole on.

EgoCycle

G ym Checklist: Get in. Get Saladin in. Bathroom. Don't chase the flowers.

We get to the Max Muscle, and we all have the same thought: I need to shit. The BDs didn't fuck us on time, so both Rita and I still have about fifteen minutes before our class begins. Rita and I head through the main entrance, a fifteen-foot armored cage that leads into the building, flanked by pillboxes. Our badges open the inside cage. We hear the staccato cracks of the roof rifles lighting something up. Sometimes our BDE syncs will count these as a kill for us, but not today. We don't see what it is, but it doesn't matter.

Once inside, we rush to the locker rooms. I make my usual detour, cutting into the custodial closet to pop open the rarely used door reserved for the cleaners to come in. Saladin is waiting, and as usual, he almost falls through the doorway, his back pressed against it, his pistol up and scanning. He is so exposed out there, but I can't get him inside any other way.

He holsters the sidearm and laughs. We both rush to the bathroom. It is a luxury, and I would be lying if I did not admit that the reason I dealt with this whole Spin hustle was that it at least gave me a place to shit during the workday. You can't put a price on comfort.

He finishes first today, and I can hear him tapping on his phone. His brother runs a Fix-It-Fast franchise, and while he can't afford to bring Saladin on full time, he does give him some part time work. This is where Saladin goes before we meet up again to do our BDE rounds. During the really lean times, Saladin will just stay here and camp the roof with the automated defenses. Maybe one out of ten would ping for him, but that was better than nothing.

"See you in a few," Saladin says as he leaves. "In sha' Allah"

"I hope so," I reply.

Once I finish (the super mega-pack of mini pizzas were not the best idea last night) I wash up and get to my station. I pass through the open area, the free weights and the treadmills. There are the regulars, the influencers, small-time comedians, and the usual youthful sort you expect to find in a gym. Some are working, taking turns with a partner recording their movements, their sets, never doing so much weight to break the perfect image. Makeup isn't cheap. The real fitness and body builder types splash water on their face, making it look like they are dripping. Unfortunately, pretty much all of them here are not that successful. I recognize a few, but there are better gyms specifically designed for streaming, but they charge a hell of a lot more, so if these folks are here, they haven't made it yet. I go here to make money, but this is the hardest. It's the job that makes me think too much.

I get to my cubicle with five minutes to spare and set my avatar. I strip off the BDE gear since all told it is about forty pounds, and I was not about to up my workout like that. The nice part of doing the EgoCycle is that it keeps me in decent shape, but I have no desire to get monster like Rita. I enjoy my svelte frame.

Once the gear is off, I get onto the bike, and I take a quick look at my clients. I have an audience of several hundred—a bit low, but this is the earlier class, mostly work at home types. The Fit Lunch crowds are generally bigger, especially since the general workday ends early on a Saturday, so people feel like they really accomplish something by hitting the cycle on the last day of the work week.

I try to get a feel of the crowd. My hands swipe through their profiles. I can be whoever I want to be, but it is not about me, it is about them. For some, they want the ebony god, a titan of muscle screaming at them to get their blood up. For others, they want the pin-up, perfect smile that is inviting, a low-cut top that is just two clicks shy of offensive. Some, they want some funk in it, kooky hair and eccentric eyes.

After about a minute, I punch up one of my standbys. It isn't the biggest crowd pleaser, but I have a healthy mix, so I need something as inoffensive as possible. I go with the tall, preppy cat with straight teeth, strong jaw, and only slightly flamboyant. The room goes dark, the screen illuminates my face, and I see the small pop-up of what I am broadcasting, another person's face that speaks something like me. When I open my mouth, so does he. When I close my eyes, so does he. He looks nothing like me, but then I don't exist anymore. I am not perceived; therefore, I am in a state of constant possibility. They only see what I want them to see. I begin to pedal.

"Ok, Cycle Cool Cats, let's earn that weekend!" I shout to my empty room. The sound is digitized and sent to several hundred rooms, a community of people entirely alone. "Show my ears that you're awake!"

"Wooooo" fills the room. Everywhere in front of me, several hundred tiny boxes of light appear. I focus my eyes on one of the boxes and suddenly the wall becomes only a single body on a machine, their face somewhat blank, somewhere between bored and empty. He can see that I am now directly viewing him, and his legs begin to pump. The hours of sweat, the rejection of simple pleasures, all of it a currency for this one moment of observation.

"Let's start it off right with some quick Courier Sprints, yeah?"

"Woooo" is the return. I adjust their bikes to low tension, but I peddle on them fast. The room around me turns into a snarl of cars, busy streets with busy lives. We are zooming between the cars, turning and banking as we move through whatever generic city the system chose to create. It sort of looks like New York. Everyone thinks of New York anyway. I'm a Cali Cat, but it's not hard to see the appeal. Even now—skyscrapers swarming with BDs, highest daily death toll in the country—it still captures the desire to be lost and found.

I have three classes today, and another gig to shift after, so I am not about to burn out before noon. I'll need to do some hills where they will burn and I will be catching my breath.

"Alright, let's get a good burst going then time to enjoy that sweet flab fire." I keep pushing them to pedal harder, some of them lost in the world, moving their bodies as if they are really dodging street signs and opening doors. After another few minutes, I can see the fatigue.

"Alright, let's cool down for a second, enjoy some eye candy, get into our soul grooves, yeah?" I say as the background turns to rolling green hills, blue sky, and fields dotted with wheat or corn or whatever the fuck it is supposed to be. I think most fields just grow soy now. The energy of the class drops, but you have to get down to get up.

I hear the ragged breathing, the grunts, the heavy glugs of water. Good. People pay to get tired, and they pay to get tired out by a professional. They need to be made to feel good. They need to be made to feel ashamed of their weakness and exalted for their strength. It's hard not to think of Dad in these moments.

My clearest memories of him are always here, on the bike. Sometimes it starts with the simple reminder that if he had just gone to a place like this, he'd still be alive. If he had just bought the damn smart bike and dealt with another monthly note, he'd still be alive. If he just stopped eating the donuts and gummies that he "bought for me," he wouldn't have had a gut to lose. If he just loved his body the way I loved him, he would still be alive.

Didn't matter in the end. Maybe we are here for a good time, not a long time. He could lift a bar and watch it bend with the weight on the end, but it didn't mean shit when he got blindsided by some genetic aberration designed to cause mayhem. Between his weights and his guns, he was waiting for shit like this, but then he wasn't around for the party. I can't help but wonder if Mom would still be alive if he was. I can't help but wonder if maybe I'd have gone to college or we would have kept a house. I can't help but wonder if I should be angry at him or just mourn him. I can't help but wonder what flowers he'd try to find even in the middle of an apocalypse that became too expensive for everyone to care.

I am crying, but they can't see that. I finish the class and do the usual bullshit.

"Thanks so much for joining me on this journey, you lovely, lovely people. Make sure to give stars for your star, likes for your love here, and come on back. I'll miss you."

Once the session is over, the room returns to light and I return to myself. I sit down on the rubber floor and rub my legs, trying to remind them that we have two more classes. I try to remind myself to endure. I get up, fill up my water bottle from the small fountain and drink. Another perk of the job is free water. I can drink as much as I want right now, but the last class, I can't. Can't afford to be on BDE rounds and worrying about taking a piss.

The next two classes are a bit more high energy. They go well enough, the same routine. For the Fit Lunch, composed of mostly men, I go with saucy, large tits, short shorts, and far more encouraging. They want to ogle you and they want you to lie to them that you enjoyed it. They want to consume that you've built your existence on their validation. I get plenty of tips this class.

For the last, just for the shake up, I go with Mom.

I probably shouldn't have named the avatar that, but it is what it is, and the gym would charge me to rename it, and well, Mom of all people would be mad if I suddenly lost a few bucks for simple vanity. She doesn't look like Mom. They are the same color, same hair, but this woman is leaner yet softer. My mother was never petite in the way that other people wanted her to be. She had wide hips and never felt like that required an apology. Her eyes were copper and salt, and when she smiled, you swear she was a different person. She was hard because she had a hard life.

Nana never talks to me about it. Mom never did either. Sometimes, usually when Mom would chew me out, she said things like "Child, you are blessed that I'm a better man than my Daddy" or "You must think the back of my hand looks fucking delicious." She never actually followed through with this, but then she didn't need to. When I was six, she had lost her temper once with me, and she pulled me so damn hard that she nearly took my hand off my wrist. She apologized over it, and I remember getting a lot of ice cream for a while when I had the cast, but that fear never left.

She had a therapist for a bit while we could afford it, and I would try to snoop in and listen to their vid sessions, but Dad was usually there to sweep me away. My folks fought bitterly sometimes; and at a certain point, they stopped caring if I could hear them. Dad would bellow out his grievances, and Mom would be on the opposite side of the room, her hands on her hips or if she had them, pockets. Sometimes, Dad would get so worked up that he'd take a step or two towards her, but he knew. He knew not to push it because he knew that if Mom started walking forward, that would be the end of it. Maybe they'd both be alive if they had gotten divorced. I'd rather have had two of every holiday than have them both be only angry memories.

They didn't usually solve things. But then, there were always flowers. Mom loved lilies, and Dad never let me forget this.

My Mom avatar works for some people. I'm like her, warm but motivating. Rage and love. Sorrow and joy. I criticize hard, and when the pretty-girl wannabe social-media fitness celebrity starts to slack, I chew her out.

"For a girl with alotta pretty ass, you aren't using it right now, ya know?" She snaps to attention and gets up into her thighs to pump hard. I smile like a wolf, and I move on to the rest of the class. True to form, just like Mom, I criticize hard, but I praise harder.

"There's mi corazón, working harder than anyone else but Jesus," I say as a younger man, barely out of high school, body built out of comfort and food that comes out of resealable bags, pushes himself so hard that he is already dripping sweat. He is trying, bless him, he is really trying. "Keep going, babe. You got this. You can do it."

She used to smother me with that. Even during the First Migration, stuck inside, looking over old pictures of Dad, she would still be there, loving as always.

"Don't put this blame on yourself, babe," she said. She knew how I felt.

"Was he always an asshole like that?" I asked. It felt good to hate him then. Hate was easy to feel, easy to use. The missing him part was what fucked me up.

"He rarely thought before he opened his mouth," Mom said, smiling and crying at the same time. "At least you knew where he was and how he stood."

"Guess it's the end of the world, huh?" I asked. I was fifteen. The country was being invaded by genetic weapons, and already, there were thousands upon thousands dead. Millions without jobs as the government floundered to figure out a way to live with it all. It felt like the end. Lots of people said so. Only Mom didn't.

"No, babe. No." She looked at the boarded-up window, just a crack left to see outside. "You are strong. You are smart. You got the best of your Daddy and me, and we both came from long lines of good people who had to endure bad days. We only think the world ends with us because it is scarier to remember that it will always keep going after you."

"If I got you, then sure," I said. She stood up, and she took me into her arms, and she breathed me in deep.

"As long and as strong as I can," she whispered.

I always remember that. I like to think of them as her last words to me. She died a year after that, and her last words were much less interesting: "Don't take me to the hospital." Pragmatic, but not wise.

It was a heart attack, I think. That's what the internet said at least. It was likely mild, and if she had gone to the hospital, they could have saved her. She was walking around and talking for a while after the initial scare, and then, she just faded away. As far as deaths go, there are worse.

Nana took it bad. I don't have any kids, and I don't know if I could ever meet anyone that would make me want them, but I know how much parents love their children. Nana cried for days. Then she just stopped. She picked up a few books from a decommissioned library, and she learned to code. Thanks to her, we're still here. We're still good.

No flowers anymore though.

I sigh and start to get the gear back on. I am tired, but I've had my time to think my thoughts, and now it is time to earn some money. Rita and Saladin will be waiting.

BDE

B DE checklist: Armor up. Phone charged. App on. Stay alive.

Rita is already outside of my pod, fully dressed. She is guzzling a protein drink, and her arms look twice as large as the last time I saw her. She has that look in her eyes. A client must have pissed her off, bad.

"Let's kill some shit," she says to me. I nod and pulse Saladin to meet us at Deductible. He is already there, hiding underneath. He must have been dropped off early.

"Safer to wait next to the cage where the guards and cannons are," Rita says.

Saladin laughs. "Maybe for you."

He opens the door for Rita and makes a gallant bow. We load up and get the scanner on the main display in the truck.

"So, any clusters?" I ask. Rita surfs through the app, and Saladin scans through the neighborhood defense apps. Those are often worthless as any loud pop suddenly turns into ten different "is that a Goliath?!" posts.

"Not at the moment. We can either skirt the boonies or try our luck and go deep," Rita says. She chews her bottom lip. She has an idea, but she doesn't like it. This means we won't like it, but it will be the best idea we got.

"Well, let's hear it then, girl," I say.

Some days, you just drive around or find a cool place to park and wait, but that burns time and gas, two things that aren't cheap.

"One of the coger-boards has been lighting up lately," Rita begins. Coger-boards were rarely used by anyone under sixty or with full bars of reception, but they ate little data, and they load on your phone even miles into wastelands. "There's a town about two hours out, been getting hit hard by packs, actual packs of Hellcats and the like."

"Telhas teeze," Saladin swears. "That's a big gamble."

"It's a lot of gas, Rita," I add.

"Three different boards have posts about it today. We could get there right at sundown, prime hunting time. An hour or two of patrol, then head home." Rita is sure. She isn't making a bigger fight about it.

"What if it is actually heavier stuff?" Saladin asks. It isn't cowardice; it's responsibility. His family loses everything if he goes down, and he knows it. You can't order a real knight in shining armor through a fuckin app.

"Between the shotty and the rifle, we should be able to handle anything," Rita says. She takes out a small clump of clay with wires. "I got this from my cousin: grade A construction demo-charge."

"Shit. Should warn me about that in my car," I say. Last thing I need is to lose Deductible. I can't code worth a damn to get any other job out there.

"Look," Rita begins. "My mom is sick. I want to take her to the doctor, but I can't if I don't have a good payday." Rita sighs. We all know that feeling. We all know what needs to be done, but we all know the pain of having to do it. We all know the reality.

"I'm in," I say. Rita needs help, that simple. Saladin lets out a somewhat exaggerated sigh.

"Together, yes?"

"Together," Rita says.

Saladin smiles and then settles into his seat. He changes apps on his phone, and texts his wife. I'll text Nana when we get out of the city. She hasn't made me dinner in a while, but just in case she starts, I don't want her to worry.

The drive out of the city isn't too bad, all told. Traffic is heavier than the morning, but once we pass the first layer of boonies, it's mostly easy going. Big armored trucks go by, taking whatever shit needs to go wherever, and those things don't stop for nothing. This is one of the hazards of taking off into the interstate. The AI's on the trucks have different protocols in the city; programmed to drive safer, smarter. Out on the lonely interstate where no one reasonably should be, they are all about speed and the protection of their cargo. When you got eighty tons moving at seventy miles an hour, there isn't a BD alive that can take that hit without being something to wash off the catcher on the front. This also means they will plow your car off the road. I don't want to lose Deductible like that.

Nana texts me back: Be safe. Be strong.

After an hour, we are getting closer. We don't have a specific pin, just the custom one that Rita collected. We exit the freeway and head up a lonely road into the mountains. Plenty of people still live this far out, away from the cities, away from the boonies. Out here, the world still mostly looks like it did twenty years ago. Grocery stores have people working in them, not security guards. Gas stations don't have armored trucks protecting them. BDs are around, and they could get bad, but BDs mostly hit the cities and boonies because that's where the big meat is. Our city has over a million people in it with another fifteen million living within an hour's drive. Where we are going, maybe ten thousand people live in the entire area, twice the size of our city.

The problem with the wastelands is when BDs hit, they hit hard. Towns like where we are going have maybe a few deputies, and usually a town militia, but they don't have BDE, they don't have constant satellite imagery, and they don't have updates about sightings. If you actually find a Goliath in sha' Allah the monster love-child of an elephant and grizzly bear—you can't call in a drone strike for 75% of the bounty with any hope it'd arrive in time to save your ass. That's why Nana and I moved.

I had just finished high school, and besides being thrilled about no longer having to take a bus for three hours round trip to get to school, I was looking at colleges. I wanted to study theater. Seems dumb now, but the world always needed stories, and not all stories could be told through a screen. I figured I could work for a year or two, save up some cash, and then enroll somewhere, get a few jobs to help supplement. Nana was supportive, like always.

We were living in a tiny town, maybe five thousand people all told. The town was broke, only a few businesses open and just one gas station. The first Migration had hurt it hard, mostly from the economic fallout rather than any particular BD swarm. Everywhere, people were out of work, and there was money going out but none of it coming in. The streets were safe from BDs, but people started getting desperate, and suddenly, you got looting in places that liked to pretend looting only happens in big cities.

Nana didn't have to pay a mortgage, but she had property taxes and utilities and food for us, and there was no work for me to find. She was working on getting her certificates, but she had to save money for the tests. We were bleeding cash bad, and her social security had ended a long time ago.

Then the swarm hit. They were mostly Garbage Geckos and a few Hellcats, but they found the town, and then it was like the first Migration all over again. People locked in their homes, constant gunfire, never knowing what was trying to chew through the door. You had to sleep in shifts because those bastards could always find a way in. They weren't smart usually, so they would hit our bottle and can alarms, but if we were both asleep, that was more than enough time for them to do what they needed to do.

We slept in the bathroom. The person on gun got to sit on the toilet, which was mildly convenient, no lie, and the person getting their rack time slept in the tub, padded with old quilts. I had Dad's pistol and his shotgun, and that was enough to keep us safe for a time, but still, bills kept coming due. We could have taken an emergency government loan, but Nana was too smart for that. She wasn't going to pay 25% interest on that shit.

She sold the house to a farming corp, and what little we got covered first and last month's rent at our current place. So there it was. I started working on my Guard Card, and I started picking up whatever gig fell in front of me. And now, here I am, going back to the wastelands. Fun times.

"I got service. Got a ping," Rita says, a bit more excited than she intended to be I think.

"From the app?" Saladin asks.

"Yep. Confirmed BD activity in our area. Got us a Sat-image, too. At least ten. double bounty."

"Fuck yeah," I can't help but say. If we get even five, that's a week's worth of pay in a night. "Any tags on them?"

"No tags confirmed, only bodies. Definitely not Geckos though," Rita continues. "We're gonna have to ear to the ground it."

"Time to get chilly then," I say and I get out the cigarettes. We only smoke when we know we are going to see something. We're all tired, up since dawn, now in the dusk, and we have to hunt. There are pep pills and shit that are way healthier, but they are expensive, much more so than Rita's homegrown tobacco. Cigarettes also don't make you piss like coffee does.

We each take a cigarette and wait for the electricity to hit our veins. We pull over at a turnout with several hundred yards of empty farmland and enough light to see through the dead grass, and we each take turns pissing, two on guns, one on nature. Then we saddle back up and drive, Rita still on the app, the reception cutting in and out. We can see some lights in the distance. Not many, but enough to be a town.

Armor. Guns. Loaded. Extra ammo. Med kit. Texts to family. Prayers to whatever. Live in the moment.

We ride into town like we matter, and there is nothing to greet us. The main street is closed down, the stores boarded up and the few that are actually still in business have their security sheets down. There are no streetlights working, but something moves on the rooftops. Saladin calls them out.

"Hellcats then," he says.

"Maybe. Fast for sure, but could be something else," Rita warns.

"Time to meet the locals," I say as we approach a gas station. There's only one way in or out, the rest protected by several layers of chain link and razor wire. There are lights on and the flashing pulse of an Open sign. I pull into the driveway as four men and three women, all with shotguns, watch me. I put my hands out the window.

"Howdy. Biological Divergence Extermination here," I say. The group exchanges glances, and one woman, the oldest, comes up to the driver's side.

"What brings you out here?" she says. I can smell the fresh blood on her. It's under her clothes, but it's there.

"We were alerted to a potential infestation, and we're here to clean it out." I smile. I try to look professional and intimidating at the same time. The pink mohawk doesn't seem to do either for her.

"Where's the rest of you?" she asks.

"We're all you need, Ma'am," Rita pipes in. The woman looks her up and down for a moment.

"Suit yourselves," the woman says. "The damned Slimeants killed at least twenty so far, injured half as many."

"Slimeants?" I ask. That's a new one.

"Bout the size of a big, big cougar, all black, have a poison in their mouth that paralyzes, look like ants up close but fleshy, like an animal," she says. She's seen one up close, but she didn't kill it. It killed someone of hers. "Sharp claws, smarter than the usual trash we find."

"Tozz Feek," Saladin whispers. I try not to show any emotion.

"Well, we could use some gas and some directions. Maybe a snack or two," I say, trying to smooth things over. Little towns always need some money coming in.

"Welcome to gas. You come back here, we can talk about something to eat," she says. She nods and a younger man comes up and starts to fill the tank. "There's a few that like to stalk main street on the rooftops. After that, best bet is off the main road towards an old quarry. We are pretty sure they nest there.”

“Well, here's for the gas, and see you soon,” I say as we finish filling up. I turn Deductible out of the gas station, and I look at Rita.

“So we gonna actually try to hit Ripleys or are we all smarter than this?” I ask. Saladin does not smile. Rita chews her lips.

“With the bonus, a single Ripley is one heavy,” Rita says, doing the math in her head. “Each.” At this, Saladin's smile slightly returns.

“But these are Ripleys,” I continue. “We've never had to deal with one, and from all the stories, I don't want to.”

“Even just bagging one or two sets us up nicely,” Rita says. “Plus, if there is a whole colony here, how long you think this town will last? How many more are gonna breed, and how many more are going to get back to us eventually?”

“Fuck me,” I say. She's right. Ripleys breed fast. All you have to do is drop one Queen with a few fertilized eggs, and she'll do the rest. They just need to eat. While no one ever says for sure, the general consensus is that Charlottesville got wiped out by a colony. The government had to actually firebomb the whole area to clear it out. Out here, no one is going to come and help until it is already bad, until the daily death tolls start hitting the news.

“Ping the app. Let's get backup. We're supposed to report Ripleys anyway,” Saladin says.

“No service,” Rita replies.

“Then we drive off to get service,” I say. “I'll eat the gas money, guys. I will.”

"Sun is dropping. They'll be coming out more and more, and it'll be harder to see them. Even if we ping, we won't have any other BDEs for hours," Rita says. "Now or never."

"What do we do?" I ask, mostly defeated. I don't want to die, not today. Some days, but not today.

"They like high ground when they hunt. Let's get up there and take it from them," Rita says with a smile. She's ready for this.

I park Deductible next to a building with an easy to reach fire escape, and we load up. Rita goes out and up first, the rifle in one hand. She practically jumps up the fire escape, relying on just one hand to pull herself up, the gun always forward, always ready. Saladin goes next and then me. We get to the rooftop, and we make a triangle: Rita looking out with the rifle on a corner, me on the right by the fire escape with the shotgun, Saladin behind us with his pistol, watching our back. It isn't perfect, but it works.

The light is fading, the sky turning bright orange and red. Ripley's are thick with a thin coat of slime. It helps them squeeze into spaces far too tight otherwise. Didn't help it's also highly corrosive for humans. The orange light cascades over the dying town, and on the roofs, Rita sees the orange reflect off a biological geometry, and she fires. Two hundred yards maybe, maybe a little less, but we hear a screech, like an eagle mixed with a fucking nightmare, and a Ripley rears up out of its place in pain. Without hesitation, Rita sends three more rounds into the beast. It screeches and screeches, but each one is softer until we no longer hear anything.

The screech is answered by several more when it falls silent. Another in front of us, one behind us, one to the side. Ripleys aren't like other BDs that mostly ignore their own kin. Ripleys are a hive creature. They understand family, and they know a threat to one is a threat to all. They also know this wasn't a fallen warrior in the hunt; they now know that they are being hunted.

"Incoming," Rita whispers. "At least we know how to bait them."

"Not fucking reassuring," I respond.

We listen. We live in the present. A few crows move from tree to tree, too scared to caw. The hushed conversations at the gas station, the light breeze carries just a shred of them to us. The slight rattle of something moving in a building. The almost imperceptible hum of our phones, of the satellites in the sky, the airplanes thirty thousand feet above. Then the rattle below me grows just a bit. The sound of something sharp, strong, scraping ever so gently against the metal. I try one last list:

Chamber hot. Safety off. Ear Buds set to combat. Live in the present.

The scraping hits again, and this time, I lean myself over the edge, barrel first, and there it is. It has the face of a primate except for insect mandibles, canine teeth, and oily, vinyl skin. It has two eyes, almost human in their hatred. I yelp out of instinct, out of the primal fear to see a predator that is your apex, and fear has me pull the trigger. I did not shoulder the gun well, and it pushes me back a bit, but the buckshot hits true. The Ripley is screaming with whatever throat it has left. I lean back over and put another two rounds into it.

"Mag change," Rita says. I still have two rounds left in the magazine, but she's right. Better to have five. Larger magazines are legal again, but damned if I could afford them. In retrospect, I should have just splurged for it. "Contact!" Rita barks as she begins to fire. "Two on the opposite buildings. 10 and 3."

I can't see the two that she is firing on, but it doesn't matter. My shotgun is worthless at this range, and my job is to try to make sure they don't get to the rooftop. There are more pops from Rita's rifle, our earbuds blocking out most of the sound. We have them set for hunting, so they exaggerate the little details and mute the louder ones. I can hear the shell casings hit the roof, but the 160 decibel report of the rifle just sounds like a cartoon.

"Behind!" Saladin yells. One scaled the building behind us, and maybe it only noticed Rita and me, not expecting the third. Saladin fires, the heavy caliber pistol making a deeper pop. I hear the Ripley scream, and I turn to put one blast into it. It's six limbs are kicking weakly in discordant directions, bleeding its strange, gray blood onto the rooftop. Saladin takes a quick picture with his phone, for the payment. "Reloading!" Saladin calls out.

"Fuck!" Rita returns. "Reloading!"

"Fuck," I whisper. Now it's just me, and while Rita can mag change and be back to her original firing position in under three seconds, it still means that my four shells have to cover all three of us. Saladin never bought those damn speed loaders like I told him to last year. He is swearing, fumbling to get the bullets out of his pocket and into the revolver. I turn back to scan the fire escape, and one is charging up, moving faster than any animal has the right to move. I squeeze the trigger out of reflex, round after round, even after it starts to fall back into the street.

I hear Rita's pops return. I turn back to check on Saladin, and he is still there, his pistol up, shaky, but up, and he is watching for anything else trying to sneak through our back. I try to focus and remember how many shells I just fired. I only have one more loaded magazine, and the extra ammo is all in Deductible. I look over the edge once more, and that's when I feel the claw.

Right up through the goddamn roof. One went into the building, and somehow, the fucker could tell exactly where I was. The roof is cheap, and Ripleys are a lot fucking stronger than they should be. It feels like having your foot caught between a curb and a car. Suddenly, that vice is pulling me down through the roof like a riptide. I hear the wood cracking, straining against the force. All I can do is point the shotgun down and fire.

The vice lets go, but another two claws reach up in retaliation. Then the roof gives, and I fall. I hear the Ripley snarling, perhaps caught off guard by the sudden rain of cheap wood and my dumb ass. Wind leaves my body as I hit something hard. My eyes can't make sense of what is going on. The sudden darkness of an abandoned building, the dust and dirt swirling in the air, the scent of gun powder and the strange menthol odor of the Ripleys. I still have the shotgun, but as soon as I try to sit up, it is the only thing between me and the mandibles.

I tuck my knees up to protect my stomach, but I can't push the damn thing away. Its claws are wild, swinging from side to side, trying to gut me. The Kevlar and plate are holding, but not for long. The mandibles chitter, desperately trying to find some piece of my face. I push as hard as I can, and my hand goes down to my thigh. The gun is there, and I don't bother to fully unholster it. I simply press the trigger.

Did I remember to put a round into the chamber? Dad was always on my ass about that.

"It doesn't have a safety. Keeping one in the pipe is asking for a bad day, Corazón," he said to me when he was showing me how to use it. The shotgun and the pistol were his last gifts to me. He bought them to "calm us down" as he would say when we'd watch the news and hear about reports of strange animal attacks. He tried to teach me, and he was mostly successful. Mostly.

The bullet hits the Ripley in one of its shoulder joints? I don't know what the fuck you call it, but where one of its arms meets its body, and it is enough for the beast to leap back in pain. I fully draw the pistol and unload the mag into its face. Out of sheer instinct, and mostly Rita's training drills, once the mag falls, I grab the extra off my hip and reload.

"Breaching!" Rita yells as she crashes down from the roof and into a deep squat. "Clear!"

Saladin lands right after her, and they are both scanning the room.

"Can you walk?" Saladin asks as he lends me a hand up. He needs to pull a lot harder than either of us want to admit, but I get to my feet. I try to put weight on my left foot, but it screams. I try again, and it hurts, but when I put pressure on it, it holds.

"Reload while we can. We need to get to the truck and back to that gas station to reassess," Rita commands. She takes the last of her full mags and swaps it. She picks up the empty pistol mag and pockets it. She gives a small smile as she does. I reload the shotgun, and Saladin nods. He finishes taking a quick snap of the dead Ripley, the flash from his phone our main light. He turns, and he puts one arm around me. I step, and he steps. He looks back, and I look forward. Rita is on point.

The store used to be something. Most of the useful shit has been looted or liquidated. There is mostly dust, some shelves filled with useless boxes, and a lot of blind spots. The only light is from the hole in the roof, Saladin's phone, and the small flashlight on Rita's rifle. The phone holder on my shotgun is destroyed, so I can't hold it and shoot at the same time.

"Maybe we get some of those shelves, build a ladder back up to the roof," Saladin says.

Rita shakes her head. "Roof is bad news. At least four more out there, and too many angles. At least in here, we can force them into a bottle neck."

"Still got that charge?" I ask.

"Blazes of glory deaths are for bullshit movies," Rita says.

"Maybe we punch a hole back to the fire escape?" I say.

Rita clicks her tongue and shakes her head again. "Too likely we fuck up the fire escape and we're back here again." Rita leans into her rifle as we hear something moving downstairs, a piece of cardboard slowly being pushed out of the way.

"A window is our best bet to the fire escape." Saladin lets go of me for a moment and takes out a small mechanic's flashlight. He pops it into his mouth and then puts his arm right back to where it was. Rita gives the signal, and Saladin moves forward, which for us is back.

We walk slow, purposeful. If something is in here, we don't need it to know where we are, but after the roof, I am pretty damn sure they can hear us or smell us well before they can see us. We walk, and we listen. There is Rita's soft footfalls, the balls of her feet landing first then a gentle transition down to the heel. Then there is Saladin and I's strange shuffling. The only smooth part of my stride is when I can swing my left forward, but this ends the moment I have to put weight on it. Each time I see a flash of white in my vision. Each time, I have to rely on Saladin more and more. Fuck.

Saladin's tiny light hits the wall, and he starts to scan. The windows are boarded up from the outside, so we look for the molding of the window. I rest my back against the wall. This way something won't kill me through the wall, at least I hope. I think the building is brick. I think.

Rita also puts her back to the wall, and together, we shuffle until Saladin lets out a small sound of satisfaction. He found a window. He feels around, looking for a latch. He lets out a small swear. Rita throws her light on him for a moment, and his finger is bleeding. The window's glass is smashed. That was good for us at least. One less thing to try and break quietly. We hear him gently tapping.

"Just plywood over the windows. I can cut it," Saladin whispers.

"How long?"

"Five minutes at most."

"Make it less than that," Rita says. She opens her mouth to say something else, but we all hear the sounds downstairs. The rustling. The crunch of something old. The gentle click of mandibles quivering in the excitement of the hunt. Rita moves to the other side of Saladin, the darker side outside of the small orb of light from the roof. We just have to hold. Saladin is already cutting, his heavy knife that's both saw and bottle opener working to make us an exit.

Five minutes in the dark. Saladin saws, a precise rhythm that is only interrupted by the impracticality of the tool. The sawing sounds like a parade to us, a meal bell for the monsters in the dark. Saladin is going as fast as he can, but it isn't necessarily fast enough. He stops when he hears the clang of something metal falling and the hisses that follow. The damn things spook themselves apparently.

"We need to go, now," I can't help but say. My gun is shaking. I don't want to die. I don't want to die like this, just trying to make some quick cash for no good reason. Even if I live, what then? Just do this again sometime later because what else is there? I'm never going to school. I'm never having a family. I'm not saving the world or finding a cure for BDs or viruses or greed. I am just living, trying to make money to live until I die. That's it. That's all there is. I don't want to die and have that be it.

"It's weakening," Saladin says as he starts to push against the board. We can hear it start to splinter, and Saladin goes back to sawing where the wood is holding strong. "Almost there, almost there."

"Just punch it," Rita says. We hear the wood crack and the last of the light outside floods in as Saladin falls through the window and onto the fire escape. The light fills the room with a gentle glow, and that's when I see it: the two Ripleys crouched and ready to pounce.

Rita and I fire at the same time. The two scatter in opposite directions, screeching. We winged them at least. Rita pushes me through the window, and Saladin picks me up. Rita falls back through the window, her gun still firing, but a good chunk of her face is missing. Two lines of ragged flesh, right through the cheek and out the other side. Saladin drops me and reaches for her, trying to get a hold of her armor to pull her away from the window. A mandible face comes rushing through the hole, but Saladin is ready. The pistol only fires once, and the creature slumps, blocking the exit with its body. Rita isn't screaming, but she isn't happy either. She tries to muffle her pain, and it sounds like a vacuum sucking up a wet napkin.

"Hurry! Hurry!" Saladin says as he lifts me up. Rita gets to her own feet, and she covers us as we practically fall down the fire escape. When we get to the bottom—my foot exploding in new pain as I land on it—Rita is still firing, but this time on the street. Two are waiting for us, bold as God in the road. I hand the shotgun to Saladin and open the car door, crawling my way into the driver's seat. Deductible starts right up. The two on the street pounce, but I am faster. I'm in reverse, Saladin still on the street, waiting for Rita.

Deductible is not very fast, and to be honest, it handles like a piece of shit, but it is reliable, and it is heavy. I feel the vibration of the two bodies, and then the jolt as I drive over them, but Deductible doesn't stop. I throw it back into drive and pull up right to Saladin and Rita. Both climb in. We speed hard into the gas station ahead, the group there already waiting for their own visitors.

"Well, you came back at least," the old woman says as I pop out of the car. I open the recessed trunk and get the med kit for Rita. She is breathing heavily, trying to stifle the pain. She always had a hard face, but now it's uneven. I take out the antiseptic spray and give her the codeine pill. She pushes the pill away.

She says something, but honestly, I can't tell what it is. A good piece of her tongue is missing, and I can see half of her teeth through one cheek. I spray down the wound and Saladin slaps on a bandage. It starts to foam and seal. I never skimp on the medical gear.

"How many did you get?" one of the men asks.

"You should be making sure we weren't followed," Saladin responds. The old woman nods and the rest of the bodies take up their positions around the only entrance.

"We got at least five for sure, maybe seven," I say. Rita's entire body shakes as she forces herself to stand. She raises her hands. "Ok, Rita says eight."

"How many did your fancy app say were in the area?"

"Ten to twenty," I say.

The old woman spits. "I hope it's ten."

"It's not. Still the breeder out there," Saladin says.

"She'll be in the quarry," the old woman says somewhat proudly. "Give me ten minutes, and I can have twenty people here ready to go."

"Fuck. That," I say. I look over Rita's face, watch her try to not look at herself in the reflection of the mirror. She was never vain, but then, she never had half of her face clawed off either.

"If you three can take down eight on your own, then imagine what you can do with some real backup," the woman presses. She's desperate. I get that. This is her home. These monsters came into her home and destroyed her normal. Everyone just lives for normal. Doesn't matter how fucked up it may be, so long as it is normal, and these things are not normal. They came in and they took someone she loved, and now they are taking the place where those memories live. I get that. I do.

But I am not going to die for this. I am not going to drive into a fucking place called "the old quarry" at night where my best shooter is injured, I can't run, and all I have with me is my buddy that has a family to consider. His wife, Ayaan, doesn't care for me much. Not because of jealousy, far from it, but rather because I am what I am, and while Saladin has come to Allah about it, she only ever sees me and my truck. Still, it matters fuck all what I think of her; Saladin loves her, built a family with her, and I am not ready to ask him to sacrifice that for these fucking people.

I am not going to have Nana outlive me. She does not need to bury anybody else. She does not need to end up on the street, alone, waiting to become food. Fuck. That.

"Look, I feel for you, but here is what we are going to do," I start. She takes a step back, and she already knows what's coming. "I am going to load up this truck with my friends. We are going to drive out of this town, stopping only to take video evidence of our confirmed kills, and then we are going back to reception. We are going to upload that video, alert the company that you got Ripleys, and then we are going home."

"Please." The woman is not begging, but this is as close as she's ever come to it. "Please, help us. They took my grandbabies. Who knows when anybody else is going to come here? You're here, and I promise, I promise I can get you fighters."

Rita looks at her and me. She is trying to say something but she can't. Between the bandage, the numbing spray, and the lack of equipment, she won't speak for some time. I shake my head hard, and I put my hand on Rita's.

"They don't pay us enough for this bullshit, and you know it," I say to Rita.

She sighs, and she reaches into her armor to reveal the demo charge. She hands it and a small detonator to the old woman.

"Best we can do for you," I say.

"Real heroes, you lot are, aren't you?" The old woman moves away from the car.

"There ain't any heroes," I say. "They got all bought out."

I get into my seat, and I get the truck moving down the road and back towards something like civilization. Saladin is on his phone, taking a video of the street, telling me to stop so he can zoom in on the bodies of the Ripleys. There's at least two inside the building that we can't see, but neither of us were going in there to get proof for all of them. Between the roads and those that fell from the rooftops with the one inside, seven. Pretty good all told.

None of us look back as we make our way to the interstate. I am utterly spent. I take out the nicotine gum and chew hard, trying for something like energy. After about thirty minutes, we all hit reception again, and we check in. I hear a lot of panicked Spanish from the backseat as Rita's mom sees the damage. Saladin is texting wildly. Nana sends me only one thing: Get home.

About an hour later, our phones all ding simultaneously. BDE accepts our video evidence and GPS logs, eight confirmed Ripleys. They invite us to wait for assistance. We decline. They confirm our night's payment as we log out of active duty for the night. We are all far richer than we started. Except maybe for Rita who is going to have a nasty doctor's bill, even if she does the minimum to not die of infection. Maybe, just maybe, our BDE insurance will cover it. It'll be a lot of paperwork, maybe some court, but she should be able to get the claim processed, and that might at least cover the regen-surgery to get her face back to what it was this morning.

I'll be out on EgoCycle for a bit until the ankle is better, so that's easy come, easy go. Still, maybe a week off is in order. Maybe Nana would like the company.

I drop Saladin off, his family waiting and cheering him on as a conquering hero. I smile and wave. They all eye me, their usual lack of understanding, the fear that comes with that, the curiosity, the promise of a wider world. I try to smile.

I take Rita home too, a medium security building. Her mother and brother are waiting, and there are tears. I try not to look at them. I try not to see their judgment. Maybe if I hadn't fucked up my ankle, maybe if I could just have gritted through it, she'd still be fine. Maybe they need to get over it and accept that a scar is just a scar, and Rita will be the same Rita once they stitch her cheek back together.

I pull into my garage, and I don't bother to change. I use the shotgun as a cane, and I limp into the elevator and then into my home. Nana is waiting, some noodles and chicken waiting.

"Hard day at the office, huh?" She chuckles. The deep lines of her face as she smiles hide the tears as they travel through the grooves.

"Overtime is a bitch and a half."

"Language!" Nana corrects. She helps me get the boots off. "You save anybody today?"

"Just ourselves," I say. "Best anyone can do nowadays."

Nana looks at me, places her hands on my face, and kisses my forehead. I breathe her in, and I remember my mother, my father. I remember a small house with fresh food in the oven, lilies and roses, and more often than not, I remember a lot of love.

"Babe, the world only runs when people look after each other," Nana says, and I cry. I cry hard.

At least tomorrow is Sunday, and I only have one gig.

RIG AND SPOOL

1. Rigging

If I had a pulmonary system, that bank would've killed me, liquifying the fleshy carbon into a gruel. Only the void knows how many tons of inertial force are coursing through my body, but I don't have a body or a pulmonary system. I don't need them. I bank, and the cruiser's firing solution comes back into view, a million tiny stars flowing out of the brilliant white ship, stretched long into a strange rectangular obelisk. The fighter is still on me, but it has no weapons lock. I bank again, this time skirting closer to the near constant stream of tiny shards of metal, each traveling at half the speed of light. I don't know if the fighter will follow me so close, and it doesn't. Too goddamn risk averse.

I dive and flip, bringing myself back into the fight and behind the fighter. There are hundreds upon hundreds of machines in the void, weaving and collapsing in brilliant flashes of light in the perfect dark of space. Human eyes could never track them all. I don't need a target lock. I can feel the energy coils tense, and when I release, it's like punching a bag of sand. I punch over and over, and while I don't connect, the fighter panics and banks too hard, right into the cruiser's firing lane, and then it's nothing but debris scattering into the Empty.

I feel the bleeding in my side for the first time. A little slow on the lateral maneuvers, which makes sense. Half of my stomach hangs out, but it is only pain. Pain is only a pulse. It's an illusion of the body, an evolutionary warning system that we have long since outgrown. It's a reminder that I need to push harder.

The cruisier isn't the actual target. The carrier a few hundred thousand kilometers away is. I don't have the piss to actually take out a carrier, but our own carrier does; it just needs the shot. The cruisers are in the way though, and any carrier-killer ordnance is going to get shredded by the cruiser's batteries or absorbed by a cruiser itself. There are six at least, plus another dozen smaller frigates keeping the carrier enveloped. Our own frigates have moved forward, skirting the firing solutions of the cruisers, trying to create dead lanes for our fighters to get in there. Our only actual ship killer frigate, the *Yumanzi*, is already down. The Adrabaecampi were not idiots, and when we dropped out of the Gate, they put everything into it. It cost them two of their cruisers, but it was a fair trade. If the *Yumanzi* was left unattended, it would have cleared the other six cruisers an hour ago.

I pull up (as much as up has any meaning in the 360 degree theater of war) and try to join with a small squadron. There is an opening. I hail the others, but they are just drones, dumb AI that is only following their models. They'll engage anything that comes too close, but they won't listen to me. Why would they? I'm just a dumb Terran Jack. The AI aren't scared.

The Campi sure are though. They are conservative, saving their fighters, keeping them from trying to engage both our frigates and our little birds. They are swarming around their own frigates, trying to keep us from strafing the point-defense cannons or tagging the engines. They are buying time, waiting for another battle group to emerge from the Gate and catch us jumpers down. We have our tachyon blankets out, hopefully stopping any extra-solar communication, but you never know. The galaxy has too much tek to ever think you got something covered.

I see my opening, and as the AI birds break from me to engage a few bandits moving a little too far from their own nest, I push for a full sprint. It feels like running downhill, letting gravity do the work, although of course gravity doesn't exist right now. I am running as hard as I can, and maybe whatever I'm leaking out the side of me makes their scanners think I am a dying duck, heading into the oblivion of their firing solution. I hear the click in my head:

"Nora, what are you attempting?" it asks.

I click over.

"I am a little bit busy right now," I say, "But get me a heavier bird loaded up for next round. Something with AS fists."

"That will be a considerable expense."

"Bill me," I say and shut the corridor between my brain and his. Pretty sure it was XyX, but it could have been & 7. Hard to tell since all Diduni sound the same. They couldn't help it; their language was built on an interwoven system of distinct chemical scents, aural inflections, and rhythmic flashing of lights from their eye stalks. The translation AI did not bother to create individual voices, and well, it was working overtime trying to get an ape and a snail to communicate at all. I was pretty sure it was XyX. Only he called me Nora, but sometimes in battles, motherfuckers get overly familiar.

I keep sprinting, pushing hard. If I had lungs, I'd be out of breath, but I do have a fission reactor, and it is starting to strain. I am moving too fast for my brain to actively discern, even with all the enhancements, and that's when you just trust what they pay us for: sheer fucking guts.

I bank once more, about to obliterate myself in the frigate's guns, and then I crash into the frigate, right where I am pretty sure the controller dome is. I ran a few missions for the Campi before, so I know their ships well enough. They liked to pilot through VR tethering. A few milliseconds slower than straight Neural Interfacing, but a lot safer. Wasn't so safe for them Shrimps, not this time. The moment I make impact with the ship, I can't feel anything except blinding pain. It's like slamming my body against a block of ice while going five times the speed of sound. It is so much pain that the human brain can't actually process it. It feels like my teeth are rotting away instantly while also having my toes slowly and methodically separated.

I have eyes again. I have lungs. I have a heartbeat, and it is raging at well over 200 bpm. My vision is still in full red out. I think I am raising my arm, but I honestly don't know. "Load me." I cough. I wanted to bark, but goddamn lungs, still trying to remember that they are fine. There's the sensation of falling, the sensation of every nerve suddenly over a fire. It fades slowly, and now I can see everything again. A VX heavy bomber. Nice. The Diduni are not fucking around with this trade route, not one bit.

I get the scans immediately: the frigate I just berserk'd is mostly fine, except all of its fighters are flying off in random directions. Most harmlessly crash against other ships or get shredded in the firing solutions. Hard to tell, but I killed maybe fifty, sixty minds.

I haul ass as fast as I can, staying under our own barrage, the missiles and solid shots getting shredded by the frigate's point defense. Still, with no fighters for at least a minute or two before the other frigates figure out the optimal ratio of fighters to divert, I can get around the cannons.

The VX isn't fast, but it's enough. My legs are like a beast of burden, sturdy, thick. I push, and I push hard. I have the payload already loaded on manual control. This is why they pay us. They want the guts. If those slime-trailing bastards did not call this Above and Beyond, my next TAC was going to be with the Campi.

I go bottom to top again. The Campi are an aquatic species, a genetic memory of soaring the currents at the top of the water and diving hard on their prey. Maybe that's why they don't worry about something coming after them from below. Not that there is any real science to back it up, just my own dumb connections. Still, it is nice to make the galaxy fit into neat patterns. That's all we are, pattern recognition engines driving rotting meat. That's all we apes can be. So they say.

No bandits are there to stop me, and I have a clear shot in the blind spot. A few SSM see me, but I can duck those easy enough. Plus, I don't need to survive this. I spin, dodging one missile and another. A human body, ruled by an inner-ear and a need for a natural horizon would be disoriented by it all, but I don't have those things right now.

There it is, the burnt ruins of my last bird, the small opening into the dome, the few bodies frozen in space still strapped into something. All munitions armed. For good measure, engines at full and containment off. It feels like being burned alive again.

I blink and I am back, screaming and tearing at my face, but I am back. It takes a few seconds to stop shaking, to stop biting my lip so hard it bleeds. I force my body to breathe.

Yes, lungs. There you are. You are whole. You are one. The meat is still there. You are the meat. You are the meat.

Fucking liar.

"Load me up, standard fighter," I say. Nothing happens. I look over and force my eyes to focus. I tap on the controller to my side. It hurts to move a real muscle. "Load me up!"

"Not a currently possible outcome, Nora. Command has you on neurological stress reduction status," XyX says. This time the voice is beside me. He is running our own Dome. The Diduni run dozens across any ship, for the exact reason I demonstrated. The other pilots, mostly Diduni but a few apes and even a few cats in the mix, are still in their rigs. The Diduni don't Neural Interface but VR instead.

"Get me command, then," I say. I am pissed, and XyX can see that.

"They will not take your communication, and they will tell me to sedate you." XyX shrugs, as much as a creature without shoulders can shrug. Really, he just raises part of his body up, and his eye-stalks sway a little bit.

All I can do is sit in my vat of neuron jelly and wait. We're way out of visual range, but at least there's a simulated map. I watch. All the birds, everyone in that room except me and XyX, are one of those little dots, sometimes gone, sometimes back.

One cat, a Fosi, jumps out of their vat yowling up a storm. It is spinning like a top, sputtering and coughing. It died hard out there. It keeps spinning, keeps coughing, and suddenly, the lights around its rig flash, and XyX is moving as fast as he can.

TBB, total brain blowout. There are fancier terms for it, but your brain isn't built to die over and over.

Well, most brains. Terrans seem to be the best at staving it off. We can die a hundred times in a day and be ready for another fight the next. Every part of my body knows what it feels like to burn, freeze, explode, and everything in between. There are ridges so deep in my brain you could grow real food in them. This is why every sentient comes calling for us when the shooting starts. Neural Interface is the only way to fly if you want to win, and Terrans, we'll do it every day, even twice on some days too.

They have the Fosi sedated. We'll see if it recovers. Most of the time you do. Most of the time. Sometimes, the brain just says done, and that's it. No amount of psycho-surgery is going to fix that.

"You're a flier down," I say. I pity the Fosi. This is good trade if you could get the work, but the payout isn't generous if you TBB in the middle of a mission.

"Unnecessary for you to return," XyX says as he resumes his position.

He changes my screen to a live stream of a recon drone. The frigate that I had hit was in half, two massive pieces of salvage now floating into the void, and the Campi Carrier is right there. I see the brilliant red flash, and the ship-ender missiles hit it dead bang. The white ship (the Campi love their ceramics) liquifies in space. It is almost beautiful to watch, to see the floating orbs of what was once something like metal drift in the black. Some of those orbs were sentients too. Maybe some were Terrans. I doubt it. Earthcode is to check in with any others in the area to make sure we aren't on opposite teams. There aren't enough of us left for that anymore.

The rest of the Campi battle group breaks hard and goes dark. Standard doctrine is to let them run. This isa trade dispute after all, and nobody wants the Convocation on their ass for going full tilt. The battle is over. A solid win for the snails.

"Command better not get cute about this," I warn XyX.

He smiles in that snail way, his vertical mouth rippling like a wave.

"I'm just an overloaded rural container of excrement in a chair. Do not blame me," he says.

"See you at the Canteen?"

"You know this."

I disconnect from the vat, pulling hair thin wires out of my head and spine. It doesn't hurt as much as it's just creepy. It's like a lover's delicate touch, and then the absence of it. Like empty beds on cold nights in the void. Like the lost memory of mother's kiss, a hug.

Once free, I take my towel, an heirloom from Terra itself, and I wipe away the gel. I have a fresh jumper to change into. The few other Terrans all do the same and nod.

"Ok, who fragged the frigate?" one asks. A large male, body chiseled from boredom and vanity. Well maintained since a few of the other Terrans either sheepishly cover themselves or pose for him.

"That would be me," I say.

He looks at me. My body isn't what it once was, four kids and a lot of stress eating. A lot of algae beer and whatever else made the pain in my head stop. Plus, I'm too damn busy to try and pretend like I'm not already the sexiest beast on the ship.

"Sweet moves," he says, his bravado starting to falter.

"You'll learn eventually, baby. Just listen and watch," I say as I zip up my jumpsuit and take some of the "tonic." The Diduni always give you some chalky drink after a connection. They say it helps ease the nerves back into receiving their data from the brain and not a computer. The big man chokes on it. It certainly doesn't taste good, but why would it? The Diduni don't have taste buds in any sense that Terrans do. It could taste like rotted ass, and they couldn't tell that from candy.

"Nora," XyX says. "Private comm, in vestibule 5."

I give him a wave and walk over. Somebody important had something to say to me.

"ITC 07160520 Terran, here," I say as I enter the small corner for privacy. I have a dedicated earpiece and everything, hard-wired into the internal comms of the ship.

"Considerable cost in ships on this engagement," the voice says, flat and monotone. "Considerable."

"Anybody else single-handedly take down a frigate?" I ask. A closed mouth don't get fed, as Mama always said.

"No," the voice says. I haven't worked with this Refactor before. It doesn't know, and that's not my fault.

"Then pay me what I am worth," I say defiantly. "How much longer would that battle have lasted? You already lost one frigate. I would hazard that you'd have lost another one. That seems a bit small compared to a few fighters."

"You are combative," it responds. "This is to be expected from your species."

"I am goddamn *combat effective* is what I am," I return. I'm not actually mad, but that is part of our allure as Terrans. We're battle-crazed, blood mad murderers, barely sapient, barely above the basest of predators. That's what it paid for, and that's what it's getting. Doesn't feel good to play up stereotypes, but starving in a Convocation relocation hab in some backwater doesn't feel good either. "I won't play again, and you know plenty of other Terrans gonna follow me on this, unless I can tell my folk that Diduni pay fair and pay well."

"Payment is not in question, only offsetting compensation," the voice says. It's bargaining, clarifying, That means it's scared.

"As long as I get full payment for that frigate, you can bill me for the fighters, and hell, throw in something for the flight bays' overtime." I laugh at this. No one knows what to do when Terrans laugh. No one gets our humor. That's fine.

"Acceptable. Funds transferred to designated holdings," the voice says.

I check my Logic, the armband going from a dull blue to red and back to blue. It flashes my account balance, a dozen zeroes more than it was when I woke up.

"Well thank you, kindly," I say. "Our transaction officially complete?"

"Additional employment option available. Do you wish to continue briefing? Continuation of briefing does not constitute acceptance..." the voice stammers on.

I know the drill. Definitely a new Refactor. The ones that know me, they can drop the Convocation bullshit. I have a reputation, a bad one at that, but every sapient knows that Nora doesn't go back on her word, and she doesn't get litigious. She gets even.

"I confirm that I am receiving a non-binding briefing," I respond in rote.

"Small squad tactical insurgency. Biomechanical anti-personnel equipment license required. Infiltration and sabotage. Payment dependent on percentage of material destroyed. Estimated length: one standard week," the voice says.

I almost coo. A smash job. Those can pay well when you're good at it, and I'm damn good.

"ITC 07160520 Terran confirms acceptance of assignment," I say. "Ready for transport at your leisure."

"Noted. Shuttle 3X57 will take you to Field Command at 2700 hours in Bay AX4."

"See you then," I say as I remove the headset and walk back to the flight deck.

My legs feel like they are in an ice bath, and it is hard to suppress the urge to gnash my teeth together, but all in all, I feel good. I have to burst Mama and Mag to let them know I won't be back for at least a Standard Week, maybe longer. This seems better. I always like a little time before coming home. It helps. I'm pretty sure the kids prefer it that way too.

"Nora, all is within acceptable parameters of existence?" XyX asks as he slowly makes his way to the lift. Diduni are pretty slow all told, but the moving walkways that fill their ships and their structures are convenient. I still usually walk when I can. I have to remind my brain that my legs are still there, still whole, and they hurt for reasons besides being incinerated.

"Just fine except I don't have a drink in my hand," I say as I take a very leisurely stroll beside XyX. He sort of snorts. Diduni show laughter by shaking their eye stalks and trilling.

"I am going to burst and walk though. Don't think me rude," I say as I bring up my comms for home. I hit the encryption key, careful to block my arm from XyX's view.

"Have to tell your family the good news, unquantifiable monosyllabic exclamation?" XyX says. "I am doing the same." XyX appears to be scooching along the walkway, all of his arms are moving in time, but inside whatever brainstem he has, he is composing a missive to his family. Last I heard, he has a whole new brood at home, six healthy eggs into six healthy children, an even split of two boys, two girls, and two neuls. That brings him up to forty-six.

"Hey Mama, Baby," I start, but first I disable the translation engine near my mouth. XyX and I are close, but we aren't that close. He doesn't need to hear this, and without the translator, even with his turned up, none of my vocal inflections would be converted into what he knew as language. "Finished the job, got a good payday. The update should hit all of you in a few days. Picked up a little bit of work. Probably be another Standard week, maybe more. Give my love to the kids. Stay safe."

XyX says something but I have no idea because all I smell is the strangely vinegar smell of a Diduni speaking. I motion for him to wait and I turn back on the translator.

"I just heard that Y@@ gave you another assignment," XyX says. Diduni proper nouns don't translate at all, so the translation AI simply creates a unique tag. It gets real annoying. I nod and smile a bit. "It must think highly of you. It comes from one of the oldest Diduni military families. Very, very specific about its ITCs."

"I hope that means it pays well," I say. XyX shakes his eye stalks. "I can always use the extra work."

"One day, you should inform me of what you do with your metaphoric fornication to indicate large or impressive sized fortunes."

"One day, maybe I will," I say. XyX gives me a smirk, well, a Diduni smirk. "I probably won't though. You can understand, right?"

"Sympathize, yes. Empathize or understand, no," XyX says. I get the distinct sense of sadness in this. I like XyX. He's been my Diduni contact and controller for ITCs as long as

I've been doing it. He's honest more than anything, and part of me wants to believe he really cares. I want to believe that.

"I'm Terran. I take what I can get." I laugh. XyX shakes. He is maybe the only Diduni I've met that sort of gets my sense of humor.

We reach the Canteen. Most of the other ITCs are there, drinking, eating, and gambling away their earnings already. XyX and I take up a set of hammocks and order: a high vintage algae beer for XyX, and a low vintage one for me. We click the bottles together in the ancient Terran way, and then trade bottles in the Diduni way, then we drink. We hand each other back our original orders.

"Going to finally settle at home with *B* and &&X?" I ask as I finish my first beer. It tastes like peat, and has much the same consistency, but it fills the belly with about as much protein as a kilo of muscle, and it takes some of the sting out of my eyes. My eyes still think I am going Mach 9.

"Yes, actually," XyX says. I am legitimately surprised. He's been an ITC controller for longer than I've been alive. He sees and understands my physical sign of surprise. "I understand and now experience my advanced age, very advanced age, Nora. I would like to raise some of my children. I missed out on such with most of them now. I am a Grand-sire, and I have not yet met most of my continued genetic legacy."

The translators don't generally work well with colloquialisms, but I get it.

"Makes sense. I just figured you were like me. Not enough gravity in the blood to settle down for too long." I smile. He seems happy about the decision, as much as I can tell.

"You should ponder this too, Nora," he says. He places an arm on mine. "You have four children, and Hera is almost of quasi-adulthood, is she not?" I nod. "Be with them. Even the Convocation cannot give you time again."

"Yeah, well, we'll see," I say, noncommittally. I don't like talking about home. "I'm Terran, remember? We don't do 'peace and quiet' well."

"I do not believe that," XyX says. "Most say Terrans are only evolutionarily designed for war and suffering, but no, I would like to believe that all sentience is a pursuit of peace."

"Nice story," I say. "But we're both creatures of war."

"Perhaps that is why it is even more important for us to find peace. We have harmed so many others, often purely as a form of commerce. If we can find peace, any sentient can," XyX says. He is being far more serious than I am used to. "We do not have to be this way. We are sentient because of the multidimensional energy emanating from our various neural structures. This is sacred, and what makes it sacred is that it can override simple three dimensional programming."

I hate when he gets all philosophical.

"I guess that means that you aren't running control on this next job, are you?"

"No," XyX says. The translation engine is forcing me to smell regret, which smells like old paper and dried flowers. "I return home, never to board a warship again, if causality is kind to me."

"Then more drinks," I say, and I order the best damn algae beer there is for us.

We drink for a few hours, swapping stories. We don't talk of the past much, only the future. The damn snail wants to start a dance studio. Diduni dance is a hell of a thing to behold, and what they can do with their shells is impressive. Most of the Terrans leave us alone, mostly because it is an odd sight to see a Terran talking and laughing with anyone not Terran. That goes for both sides. The time changes, and I need to sober up and make it to the bays.

"Be safe. Live a long, peaceful life, Nora," XyX says. "I have sent you my personal burst coordinates back home on Didun. You are welcome to communicate at any time."

"Maybe I will," I say. XyX chuckles. "But I probably won't." XyX gives a long motion with his hands, all four sets coming together like a bridge before slowly collapsing, the Diduni motion for farewell, used at weddings and funerals. I kiss my fingers, place them over my heart, and leave.

2. Meat

I take the moving paths because I am a little bit drunk. Holding the railing grounds me in existence. The bays come into view, and when I arrive at mine, a frigate is waiting for me. One of their smaller ones that's easy to hide in the void, runs as silent as dark matter. I'm definitely not doing a trade dispute this time.

The guard scans my body, and my ITC tag glows for a second in my hand. The doors open, and the guard, somewhat nervously, motions me forward. His eye stalks follow me as I walk in and find a chamber. I strap in, insert the various needles into their ports, and I let the machine do its magic.

I'm not asleep. I'm acutely aware of all of my surroundings, of the ship itself. My consciousness is plugged into about two dozen different sensors. I can see any room in the ship that isn't restricted. I can smell the room. I can taste the forced humidity in the air. When the gravity clicks off and the ship begins to move, I can feel it. If the pilot so wishes, I could feel the weapon systems, I could feel the metal skin of the ship. I'm an ITC, not cargo. I get to stay awake.

"Welcome Independent Tactical Combatant, 07160520, Terran," a voice says, the same from the flight deck. "Mission briefing will begin in three...two...one."

With that, my mind is suddenly flooded with information. The geological history of a small tectonic plate on a small continent on a massive planet. The evolutionary pathway of all major flora and fauna on said plate. The ancient history of the people that now inhabit it. Everything the Diduni know, I know. Then finally, the actual mission details start to bubble to the surface.

Definitely not a trade dispute. A personal vendetta. Small pirate colony, ship bay, minor satellite defenses. No registered permit to operate on the planet. No registration on the defenses. Mixture of species. Mostly provincials from the same quadrant, so the usual rag-tag group of sentients that are trying to make a living outside of the Convocation. I get it. I do. But that doesn't change the equation here.

My mind is forced full with downloaded data, the specific evolutionary track of a super-fauna, a predator. Evolved out of a rat-like entity, but at least four hundred kilos now, body covered in thick, natural armor of cartilage and subdermal bone. Massive jaws for chewing limbs whole, powerful legs, ambush predator.

"A standard INJEN stealth rig with phosphorus missiles would be a lot faster and more efficient," I say, or rather think. There are two layers to the neural network, one that I can consciously project, and one that I can suppress. It cannot hear all of my thoughts unless I allow it. It's like pushing something buoyant under water.

"Specific mission parameters: You must use the provided proxy, and you have only one," it says. "There is a factor of ten increase in payment if the proxy is either destroyed to the point of no reasonable access to its neural command node or safely exfiltrated."

"This is very much not authorized by those above you, is it?" It's not really a question. I know how it goes. A rich little snail trying to get some payback. Maybe these were some of its off-the-books operatives, and they know too much.

"Irrelevant. As an Independent, you have full indemnity for this mission under Section 127, sub-section 542, in the Convocation Treatise on Acceptable Violence," it says, somewhat annoyed. I know the damn Treatise, too. "I am the only one liable."

"But if you are asking me to commit actions that are expressly banned in Section 17, sub-section 5, then my indemnity is void," I reply with a bit of a laugh. "So let's just make this easier on both of us and be clear about what you need me to do."

There is silence for a time, even the data dump stops. It is thinking. I'm not surprised. Terrans aren't held in much regard for our capacities in law, logic, or morality. We are only regarded as dangerous animals, suited towards violence. The Convocation only begrudgingly gave us full status as Higher Sentients because they were afraid of what several hundred thousand pissed off Terrans could do where everyone was the enemy, left alone to wreak mindless havoc in a galaxy. We had ships, and as we'd proven time and time again, that's all we need to be more than a nuisance. A good chunk of the Convocation members believed the Upi when they said we were too dangerous to live. Maybe we ended up proving them right, but we are still alive, a few of us at least.

"The illegal enterprise here is in direct competition with one of my enterprises. I need them mechanically and financially crippled, so I may acquire their market share at a low cost in both resources and time," it says.

"So you want some of them breathing after all this?"

"Yes. I want considerable damage, and I want them afraid," it says.

"But you don't want them to have any real proof that you did it," I say.

More thinking.

"Look, Y@@, is it?"

"XyX holds you in too close of confidence," Y@@ says in an almost threatening manner. I smell smoldering coals and dead skin. "Yes, that is me."

"First off," I begin. It was starting to work my last good nerve, and after twenty-three years of having my proxy bodies destroyed over and over again, this was far more accurate than I wanted to admit. "XyX is good folk who never lied to me, never tried to deceive me, and after two hundred successful combat missions, the proof is in the algae that his approach works, so try it. Second, you keep his name out of your damn vocal chords and pheromone glands. Third, I will get this job done and done right, so long as you keep up."

There is more silence. The data dump continues. They are spooling out my proxy now. He's a big bastard, sharp teeth, strong legs and arms. He has two small sets of arms, not much bigger than mine, that almost hide along his belly, delicate claws rather than the brutal things at the front and back set. The tail is particularly impressive. I do enjoy getting to play with a tail, although it takes a little bit to get the feel for. In a vehicle or suit, you can imagine the abstract functions into something relatable—throwing a punch, running, ducking for cover—but when riding in a biological, there are often limbs and appendages that have no direct Terran counterpart. It's harder for the mind to find purchase. It's too familiar yet too alien all at once.

"Any last minute alterations to the proxy before the spooling ends?" Y@@ asks. "This must be within what the creature could naturally and normally possess."

"Largest recorded was 417 kg. Make sure it is under four ten," I say. "Makes it look a bit more realistic."

"Understood."

I watch the system build the creature, muscle fiber by muscle fiber. He's the perfect specimen, aged to full adulthood but without the usual wear and tear. Born as if raised with an optimal diet down to the macronutrient. He is beautiful, and it is no wonder that the pre-bronze sentients on the planet worship them as avenging demons. I'd be worried to hunt one with a full suit on, let alone with sharp sticks and a lot of gumption. The neural command node is already in place, now being covered by the rest of the brain. I can already feel it, an emptiness where my mind could go if I so chose. My node is humming, waiting to connect, waiting to send my collection of neural energy—the only multi-dimensional energy Terrans can allegedly access—to the node.

Mama was never so sure about that. Her own mother remembered a time before Discovery, before humans met with the first representative of the Convocation. We were still trying to force bacteria to dissolve the methane on Venus or trying to get crude engines to build an atmosphere on Mars. Newtonian and Einsteinian physics were still considered absolute. Terra was burning to death. Mama always said that her mother never believed the stories about the Convocation: that there were aliens, that sentience was its own energy, the meat was just a three-dimensional way to contain it. Mama still doesn't believe all that. To her, the flesh was the Terran, and the Terran was flesh.

The only thing I know is that it was luck that my grandmother was a dirt farmer. What she taught my mother kept us alive, kept her alive after the Upi atomized Terra. And Venus. And Mars. Mama and her brothers weren't some explorer's kids, trained to fly, trained to negotiate. They were trained to live, and so here we are.

"Preparing for Gating. Stand-by," Y@@ says.

I force my node to quiet itself. Going through a Gate hurts like hell if your node is open and searching. All the minds, all the stories, all the energy of universes that you can't see suddenly screaming for a ride. The ship shimmers for a moment, everything becoming almost digitized as a three-dimensional space is converted to two and eventually one. Then there is the cold, and the return, and suddenly, I am millions of lightyears away, appearing around a giant spinning orb.

I'm lucky to have actually seen Gates with a variety of eyes. To Terran eyes, they look like small comets, but they are perfectly smooth, a shifting chroma of colors. When they open, the orb just floats there, but the colors shatter and break into a million shooting stars, and then suddenly, whatever was near the orb is gone or there is now a new ship as if it was already there.

To a ship's eyes, they are massive, far more massive than you would think, and they are constantly in motion. What was once an orb becomes a diamond, a rectangle, an octagon, and back to orb all in milliseconds. There are waves of varying radiation, and when the orb opens, it ceases to exist. Every scanner goes dead as if there was nothing there, and there never was, and there never will be. Then all of a sudden, you have a ship, and the orb is back, pulsating and shifting.

I open my node back up, and everything is fine. The ship is moving now at speed, firing up the sub-space blades, and now, physically, everything inside this million kiloton piece of metal and ceramic occupies no more physical space than a grain of sand, at least on the standard dimension of existence. In the others, it's hard to tell. Terran minds aren't built to understand the other dimensions, so they say. All I know is that the ship is moving at several factors of ten more than the speed of light.

It will be a few days before we arrive. This used to be my favorite part of any job, reclining in my pod, my body disconnected from my mind, free to let the body and mind heal. When XyX was on the controller, this is when we would chat. There wasn't much more to do than that. Of course, the manuals, the training, will tell you that this is the time to study assault vectors, run through the probabilities of each possible outcome, but that's what the combat algorithms are for. This is the time to rest, and when the bloodletting starts, then you let instinct kick in. That's what everyone called it, Terran fighting instinct.

"We are biologically designed for this," Shaun would say. He was my first husband. He was an ITC too. We met during these travel periods, waiting for the next engagement. "It is simple science: life on Terra evolved out of brutal Darwinian competition, competition built on violence. Most of these others, they came from cooperative biomes, but not us."

"There's a reason Terrans don't suffer from the TBB like everything else," I said. I was young, barely seventeen and only a few missions under me. Meeting Shaun was also the first time I met XyX.

"Curious, what is that reason to you?" XyX asked. I remember both Shaun and I were somewhat taken aback that he bothered to speak to us. Terra had only been gone for some thirty of our years at that point, and the memory was still fresh for the longer lived sentients out there. The genocide of two separate sentients, most especially the Upi, still hung like a pall over the Convocation.

"We are just the meanest fuckers in the galaxy," I said, laughing. I think part of this bravado was to impress Shaun. He was older, a seasoned veteran, and he was beautiful. I wanted him to notice me. He laughed right along with me.

"She's young and lacks a certain sophistication, but she's right in essence," Shaun said. He was the son of an explorer, the somewhat rich Terrans that somehow got access to ships before the Upi, charged with finding new resources in what was declared Terran space. There were a lot of explorers who came back to find Terra gone, so now most Terrans were either the children of explorers or the children of their servants or prisoners. Some, like Mama, were just stowaways or those who stormed the shipyards and took whatever could fly.

"Your cortexes both show early signs of neural trauma," XyX said. "It seems considerable already."

"I'm fit and fine," I said, winking, well, thinking the concept of winking, at Shaun. "Maybe that's just how our brains are normally. Ever see a non-ITC Terran brain?"

"She's right. Our brains are completely in-line with Terran biomedical records," Shaun said.

"Point taken," XyX said. "Still, logically, one should caution against such trauma. A frigate is designed to take damage in battle; that does not mean that it should."

"But by its design, it is *meant* to take damage," I say.

Shaun sends the suggestion of a raised eyebrow.

"Hear hear," Shaun says. XyX muses over this for some time.

Shaun and I spent the rest of the travel time talking, me falling in love, him pontificating. That was how it was in those early days. We even had a whole crew, a small company of about twenty Terrans, and we made a bit of a name for ourselves: *The Bondea*. Mama used to say that quite often, usually when I did something wrong, so it made sense. We were looking to do wrong and get paid for it.

Those early years, work was constant. With the Upi gone, one of the Convocation's largest and most successful factions, the power vacuum meant ITCs were in high demand, and well, if a few hundred thousand Terrans could annihilate a civilization that has lasted for twenty thousand years in the blink of an eye, sentients paid good money to have some of that raw rage on their side.

Shaun and I eventually married, cemented our hold over *The Bondea*, and we were making a real living.

Mama hated it. She hated him. He had a walk, a talk about him. Explorers like Shaun loved to say that the old hates in humanity were gone with Terra, but he wouldn't think to marry me until he was sure that Mama had come straight from Terra herself.

"Boy wouldn't know sense if it punched him," Mama said to me once. I had just given birth to Hera, our oldest, and Shaun had already taken *The Bondea* off on a mission. I had asked him to stay, to be a family with me, even for just a few months. We were still living on a Convocation planet lease, a pretty little jewel that constantly reeked of methane, but it had beautiful purple sunsets. We had enough to get by, some basic manufacturing, basic agriculture, but the times were lean, and it's not like traders or anybody else ever came by. Hell, it was a month long flight just to a Gate. Even if the mission was quick, that was at least two standard months gone.

"We gotta make money, Mama," I said, gritting my teeth in frustration, trying to get Hera to latch. "Little girl here just can't seem to take the hint."

"Slow down, sweetie. Slow down. Give her a second to get her bearings," Mama cooed.

"How'd we ever survive if breastfeeding was this hard for everyone," I said. By then, I had already gotten the dreams. Made it hard to sleep, reliving the worst battles, your body convinced that it was dying. Your mind tried to remember what meat suit it occupied, if it was even meat at all. Sometimes, I'd go numb for hours, my mind sure that my body was made of metal.

"Takes time. Not as easy as the books say it should be," Mama said. "Nothing wrong with that."

"Don't steel on Shaun when he isn't here," I said, returning back to the conversation. "Even though I know you do it plenty to his face."

"Baby is hardly a week old, and he's out there already. Don't think I didn't hear how he spoke to you when he left."

"Couples fight. You and Daddy did all the time," I countered.

"Your Daddy never, no matter how hard his brain was leaking, not once ever called me those things. He never once gave me any reason to doubt that he loved me, that he saw me as equal, that we weren't together until the end."

"Don't matter now. Won't see him for at least two months, probably three," I said. Mostly, I wanted to not think about Daddy. He would always be two men to me: the man that I saw with a child's eye, and the man that I buried.

By the end of his life, much shorter than it needed to be, he was mostly catatonic, small piles of drool out of the sunken side of his face, the TBBs giving him stroke after stroke. If he was awake, he was like a lost child. Rarely angry, mostly morose, the unbearable weight of understanding his situation dragging him to the ground.

When he died, he hadn't spoken in weeks. He finally let out a small cry before seizing in bed.

He was strong once, stood tall above everyone else not just because of his size but because of his dignity. He was the best damn ITC out there, and I can never lie and act like he didn't open doors for me.

It's hard to not think of Daddy when jacked into a biological. It's hard to maintain distance in them. The pain is real. That's what Daddy taught me: pain is universal. It is what we all share, every sentient and less than sentient. All life, connected by the hurt inside. I try to push away the memories, but they are there, always there.

The beastie is spooled, and the neural node is open. I drift into him, step inside, and no longer am I in a small tube of gel but rather I am tied down, shackled. I am a beast; no, I am not. The beast is me, and I am it.

I have the urge to run. Goddamn, this thing is so juiced with aggression hormones that it makes me want to kill every single snail on this boat. There's only one snail, and well, he's already pissed me off, but that's the meat talking. The meat has its own voice. That's what I know. The meat can sing when it wants to, and right now, this thing wants violence. It is a familiar feeling, comforting and warm.

"Get the chains off, now," I growl. The voice is in my head, but the beast struggles against its restraints and lets out a bellowing cry.

"Standard procedure. For all of our safety," Y@@ says.

"I need to get used to the ride," I say. "And I don't like chains. You got security drones if I get rowdy. "The restraints click, and I can move. It feels good to stretch, muscles designed for the hunt, spooled out into perfection, but they've never moved before. All the pathways are there, but they are unwalked. I step out of the machine, and I prowl. I am a bit clumsy at first, trying to find the balance. The tail is much heavier than I thought. It is prehensile, and it feels like a strange, powerful finger coming out of my back.

I run the halls, scarring the floor some. This thing can't turn as fast as I'd like, too much bulk to shift quickly. That said, I can feel the metal underneath flex as I push against it, and I know I can claw through a door without much trouble.

Getting used to the vision is the hardest. The beast does not see in color, nor does it see in infrared. The eyes, more like organic glass shards covering the head, see electromagnetic currents. I can see the ship, see the outline of the pulses of energy. I can even see the snail, sitting at the command deck, its arms moving around a buzzing orb of energy.

I can only see the walls by the emptiness that they create. It is as much feeling as seeing. Smell and hearing is at least five times that of my Terran meat. I can smell my own body, the strange notes of algae, alcohol, even the early start of my cycle. It is a beautiful experience.

The next few days are all the same, me running the halls, the snail ignoring me for the most part. It isn't until we reach the destination that it gets chatty again.

"You will be inserted here," the snail says, but this is all in my brain already. It is standard practice to repeat it verbally, but I hate standard practice. It is interesting to see Y@@ for the first time. We are both out of our vats, breathing the same oxygen, able to smell the other. It is pretty for a Diduni. About as long as me if I am laying flat, a good two heads taller than me at the height of its shell, a strange, purple, half chitin, half metal lump on its back, brimming with different mechanism, the strange, almost impassive face. I know them well enough to see that it is large for the species, strong and quite young. Neuls usually are larger on the account of incubating the young, but it is especially impressive. I'm sure it would say that it was due to good breeding or some such.

"I know the drill. Make sure the ride is well caloried," I say. "Sooner we get this done, the sooner I get paid."

"Again, per the contract, ensure the extraction or full destruction of the asset..."

"And you slap a few zeros on my payday, got it," I cut it off. I am in a bad mood. Part of that damn thing's bio-chemistry is to be amped up on aggression hormones at all times, and well, I guess my own meat suit is getting some inspiration. It happens. I want to kill something, eat something, and fuck something.

"We should respect protocol," Y@@ chides.

"Talk to me honestly here," I say. "You're new to this, aren't you?"

The snail is caught off guard. I figure that it is so used to its inherited station that blunt honesty from a lesser is not a daily occurrence. It is thinking; I can see the eye stalks twitch and one set of its arms absently rub its shell.

"I have studied for years at the greatest military academy in the Convocation, and my own sires have waged hundreds of years of warfare with an unassailable reputation," it says, but even my translator can detect the lack of bravado. This is an admission of weakness.

"Ok, so you're new, fresh out of schooling, and you need this to go well," I say. While Diduni cannot shuffle their feet, they do sway a bit when anxious. "That's why XyX told you to go with me."

"He was insistent that I choose you and only you," it says. "His recommendation carries great weight with my kind." I smell its discomfort, its desire to be stronger than this. It really is more of a child than anything else.

"Then listen to me. Talk to me," I say, and I can hear Mag's words in my head. "Half our hates are from not being heard, and the other half from not listening."

"Translation is odd, but I present understanding of this," it says. "What do you need from me?"

"Did your family make you do this? Is this your blooodening?" I ask. The poor thing looks at me with clear confusion. The translator can't make it work. "Is this an exercise to determine your social and/or economic value to your family?"

"Yes."

I smell sadness. I smell regret. It is burnt alcohol and ozone. It is blood.

"Do you even want to be doing any of this?"

After some time, it replies, "No. I find no enjoyment from the military arts."

"Your folks won't let you out?"

"No. As a Nuel, I carry the next generation, and so my body must be made strong through battle."

"But not actually in any rig, just operating. Just watching," I say.

It gives the Diduni version of a nod, both eye stalks moving down and then up in rapid succession.

"Sounds about right."

"I do not understand."

"You will," I say, and I sigh. I try to exaggerate such for the translators. "Listen, you just let me do what I do, and I will get this done. You feed me usable data, keep me from blowing out my nervous system, and keep me focused on the task, and we will get this done."

"I understand," it says.

I put out my two arms, palms up—the Diduni gesture for comfort. It looks at me for a moment, eye stalks twitching, but it places two outstretched arms to run parallel next to mine.

"Now let's do the job and worry about the rest after," I say as I walk back to my vat. I strip down and let the fibers insert into my nervous system. Y@@ runs through the pre-drop checklist, and my ride is fitted into its deployment pod. I give it my confirmation, and I am now in the meat, encased in darkness, the pod's hull too thick to see beyond. It feels like a cage.

"Last initiated transmission," Y@@ says.

"Communication discipline in effect, confirmed," I reply.

Y@@ counts me down, and suddenly I am falling. I feel the force of the planet's gravity, falling as fast as Newtonian physics will allow. I start to see the red lines of energy as the pod enters atmo, and then the sudden jolt as the pod's own engines start and now I am flying. It does not take long before the sensation slows and finally stops. The restraints holding me unlock, and the pod opens, revealing real air, real life all around me.

The continent is mostly jungle, thick with life. I can see everything. I can see the myriad insects in their air, their tiny bioelectric pulses filling the air like wisps of dreams. The trees are outlined in their subtle currents, and far away, I can even see the vague outline of larger creatures, all prey.

I can smell the life in the earth, the billions of unseen and unheralded components of creation. I can taste the moisture in the air, taste that somewhere not that far, a female of my meat's species is in heat, and it takes every bit of control to not go bounding in that direction.

I know where I must go, and I start out at a jog. I have to cover fifty kilometers in a short window, with strength to fight, and while the beast is perfectly capable of this, I can't push it yet. Part of me is happy to have sky above and soft earth below me. The world is an ever-shifting explosion of light, and I want to savor it. I jog, and I hear the animals fleeing. I taste their fear on the wind, and it tastes good.

After some time, I reach the outskirts of the pirate base. I see something strange, a dome of razor thin purple light all around. It shimmers in and out of existence, one moment there, one moment gone. When I focus, I can see that it is actually expanding and contracting at a speed too fast for me to process. I watch as insects flutter through it and back. I sniff the air deeply.

A perimeter scanner, decent one at that. This group is smart, or just as likely, a few of these beasts have gotten in before. I could turn on my comms, get Y@@ to fry their systems easily enough, but that would give up the game. I have to get into their base, but my best chance to do real damage is to get in there without being noticed.

The air is full of the scent of animals, and I can make something out. Judging by the amount of methane it's pumping, it has to be large. Now I stalk. It feels good to move slow, deliberate, with purpose. You can either achieve a goal or you can avoid pain, but never both at the same time. That is the simplest principle of life, and it feels good to be a part of it with little distraction.

I slowly move through the dense foliage, my belly scrapping the earth. The small arms underneath almost retract into the stomach, staying safe from the rocks and roots that would cut open the delicate skin. I can see the creatures through the jungle now, a herd of perhaps two dozen creatures, somewhere between ursine and bovine. They are big though, easily twice the size of my meat, but they aren't armored like me, and I bet they aren't as mean. I hear them sniff the air cautiously.

I circle around them, making sure that they catch my scent only when I am aligned properly. My body is hungry, having never eaten a real meal yet, and it wants to. It knows what it needs to do. I feel my body tense and then there is release as I sprint forward. The animals let out bleating cries and run as fast as they can, knocking down young trees. I am faster, and I am able to move at their flanks, snapping and clawing, keeping them on the path.

I can see the sensor wall now, and they push through with ease. I move into the center of them, scattering them as much as possible. Now I can see the outlines of the buildings ahead, the glowing epicenters of the base, and the energy shifts suddenly as their alarms are activated. I can't understand, but I hear fragments of raised voices. In the middle of the herd, I look for my chance, and there it is, an unfinished piping trench. The pirates are planning on expanding. I dash into the trench and slide on my belly through it.

When I reach the end, I hear the commotion settling down. The pirates seem content that it was just the beasts, but I smell ozone. They fired at them. I lift just the top of my head up to see clearer, without the interference of the ground, and I am near the Communications building. It is full of a blinding white light and then a huge stretch of emptiness far away to its west. Hard to land orbital flyers without comms, likely just incinerate yourself. That is the best place to go. I trust in the darkness of my skin and the night, and I sprint to the building.

It is easy to climb, and I find myself on the roof without much effort. I can see the energy outline on the doorway, some kind of alarm. There is a ventilation shaft. It would not support my weight once inside, but it doesn't have any sort of security system. I use my small arms to gently remove the grate, and I put my head inside.

With my snout in the ventilation, I can hear and smell most of the building. To keep the connection as quiet as possible, the translator is off. It doesn't matter. I can smell them all, and that is enough. I could go left and down, crashing into another room, a habitat block. There are four or five bandits there. They smell like standard protein gruel, a mixture of recycled plant matter and raw minerals. It's what you got served on most Convocation rocks when they wanted to say they fed you but didn't particularly want you to live. They smell mid level anxious, even though by the sounds of everything, nothing particularly dangerous is facing them, and they are oblivious to me. No, it's just the standard mental weight of barely getting by, wondering when a real meal will come, wondering how and where the next boot would come to kick you in the ass.

To the right, another hab, only two. The methanol and ethanol is strong on them, heavy drinkers. There's an undercurrent of skits, a dopamine and oxytocin inhibitor. It's useful stuff if you want to stop feeling anything: pain, regret, empathy. Then there's the real mineral smell, the building blocks, dead, old blood under nails, on clothes, underneath it all.

I go right.

I let the tail release, and I manage to propel myself through the shaft before my weight shatters it and I go crashing down into the hab. As I fall, I manage to reach out with one claw and crush one of the sentients in the room. He barely has time to cry out before the weight of the claw rips through his body. The other sentient reaches for some kind of weapon, but I am already moving forward. His reactions are hardened, a veteran, but I am too fast, and his weapon is too far away. I take his head into my mouth and crunch down.

The taste is electricity, a jolt to my system and I have to fight hard to keep the meat from letting out a triumphant roar. I can't stop the meat from taking large goblets of flesh into its mouth and hungrily gulping them down, and after a few bites, I stop trying to fight it. It tastes good, and the meat needs to eat after all. Plus, this has to look like an actual animal attack, and animals don't just kill; they devour. I do stop it before it eats all of the corpse, simply because I don't want a full stomach to slow the reflexes. The meat resists, but I am it, and it is me, so I must only command myself.

No, the self is beyond such simple ideas of unity or division. I stop. I breathe, and I look through the walls. There is panic in the building now. Someone heard the noise. I don't think they know what it was, but they know something has happened. I scratch at the door release, and I continue forward. I am in the halls now so speed is important. I see the glowing cacophony of the main control room for the comms, and I put myself in motion. There is no stopping now. I turn one corner, and I can see it, and unfortunately, I can see someone.

She is looking at a scanner, probably trying to determine what is happening, but she is too close for me to stop. Maybe she was a terrible bitch that didn't need to take up any space. Maybe she just got back from ordering the destruction of some minor settlement for quick cash. Maybe she sided with the Upi. It doesn't matter. Chances are, she's just a regular carbon dump like me, but she is unlucky. I crash into her and carry our weight through the door, smashing it down, and smashing her along with it. She is not dead yet, but I doubt her meat will live.

I begin the work. Mostly, I thrash around, using the tail like a whip to slice through the consoles. The talons on the inner set of arms are nimble enough to actually work the console, especially if I bother to link up with the translation engine, but there's no time now. Plus, if I overload the system and fry the antenna, that'd be expensive to replace, even for Y@@'s family. Thrashing the command nodes will make the system worthless for a while, but it's not particularly hard to fix, given the time and resources.

The energies around the building surge and sputter before dying, and as the cricket-woman I smashed through the door gasps her last breaths, so too does the communication systems in the entire settlement. They'll likely have small backups all around to ensure immediate communication, but there is no way for any space-faring vessel to land here now without likely incinerating a building or two. With some of the static gone, I can see the other buildings, several coming to life more and more. I also see two bright bursts of light, so much energy that it's almost impossible to see their outline. Exosuits most likely.

A standard exosuit is a significant investment for a private outfit, and for good reason. They make a single combatant dangerous to almost any planetside material that might be present. I can't make out their shape, but I move fast anyway. I can see the waves of energy hitting all around me, illuminating everything in the building. They are scanning. The whine of machinery, the pop of tension being released, and the zing as kinetic weapons rip through the walls means they found me. I push as hard as I can, crashing through walls, searching for something strong enough to stop their munitions, but there isn't much that will.

I crash through a wall and make it back to the outside. The meat rejoices at the real atmosphere. I can't enjoy it. I run as fast as I can, weaving to avoid target lock, watching the strange halos that their weapons make, hearing metal pass by me, smelling the burnt combustibles. I have to make it to their dry dock. A space-faring vessel could take those hits, give me some cover. I want to check in with Y@@, but with exos on me, their systems could likely detect the link and then it's all over for the bonus.

One of the exos is moving to flank me. Smart. All I can do is trust the meat. I put every thought into moving, and I am in full sprint. I ignore the burning muscles, the lack of oxygen as the lungs work beyond their normal capacity. Pieces of my flesh disappear as the shower of kinetic weapons hone in closer and closer. The one moving to flank me is the most immediate concern. My only hope is to be faster than it.

I can see the faded outline of a ship, most of the systems powered down except for the essential. I am almost there. Then a piece of my tail explodes and flies away. It takes everything in me not to stumble and fall without the weight to balance my stride. Perhaps if I wasn't used to running without a tail, my mind couldn't have done the math to make that possible, but I stay up, and despite the pain, I make it into the massive building. The firing stops as ricochets fill the space. They are not interested in damaging one of their ships. This becomes my best hope. No more exfiltration now, just death, but I need fireworks.

I pry open the rear loading door on the ship, a standard orbiter used to ferry materials planetside to voidside. This will not be an overly expensive loss, but a vital one nonetheless. For the sentients living on the fringes, this is a treasure, and I understand that well. My own personal vessel wasn't much, but if I didn't have it, I wouldn't have been able to do much. Hard to make a living without a way around, and as much as a rock jumper like this was a century too old and barely a line item on a financial report to most folk, it's what held their world together. I feel bad for what I am about to do. I really do.

I make my way to the engine, and I start to chew. Without full power in the system, it won't blow, but I'm not going to be the one to rupture it. I make noise, scream, roar in defiance, all while destroying any system dedicated to safe containment. A standard fission engine won't fully meltdown unless you push it hard and have all the safety systems turned off, but it can bleed radiation, and that is what kills you. Sometimes, it's enough radiation to melt the ship itself. The coolant is also highly flammable, and it burns as hot as phosphorus, so it helps to have it covering everywhere.

I continue to thrash, to cause a ruckus, and outside, the two exosuits have a choice: wait me out and let me destroy their ship, or try to save it by coming in after me. They choose the second option because the ship is too valuable to lose. Their sensors should show the huge spike in radiation. My meat's internal organs are starting to cook. The connection becomes jerky, dulled from the radiation as it starts to fry the implant. We are all running out of choices.

The two suits enter the ship, unaware that I can see them as they can see me. I stay by the engine, letting the waves of radiation soak me. I need them to come in, and I need them to hurry. I let out more cries of pain, more challenging roars, and for good measure, I continue to thrash around, tearing mostly cosmetic metal plating on the walls, just for the effect. This kicks them into gear, and they push forward. By the energy outline, they have sonic weapons primed for me, safer for the engine and ship, but not what I need. I need combustion. I need fire. Once they are close enough, all I can do is take one last good breath and charge.

They are expecting it, but they are not expecting that I am holding up what was once a blast door, using the metal to absorb the vibrations of their weapons. My bones crack under the strain, but they are holding, and I am getting close enough. I throw the door into them, knocking them both back, and I pounce. What is left of my tail controls one exo's arms, and my dominant claws control the other. I can't penetrate the armor into their flesh easily, but the less dominant arms, the feeders, can work the external controls of the exo. The exosuits are standard Convocation design meant for use with all bipedal sentients, which means by necessity, some of the commands are external, for safety reasons they say.

I wrestle with both, relying more on dead weight than actual muscle as most the bones in my body have fractures now. I scream in pain out of instinct, while the feeders do their work, and now, one of the exosuits is bleeding fluid. One of the exos wriggles free, and the pilot goes with instinct. It opens fire, hitting me broadside, but it also hits the metal of the ship. With a spark, the leaked fluid starts an impressive fire.

We are all burning now. The fire reaches up the leaking exo and into storage, and then there is a loud pop as it explodes, taking most of the exo with it, and more than half of me as I am thrown off. I am now two pieces, and I can't feel my lower half. The other exo turns and runs to get out of the ship before the fire suppression systems trigger. With my one good arm, I drag myself, my bones cracking under the strain, to place my head over the burning exo. The fire is white hot, and I feel the skin start to melt away. I push down, making sure it melts the entire skull. Then I am in a white space of pain, blinded and deafened by everything.

3. Memory

I am in a vat of goo with Y@@ looking at me, furiously working its command node, likely trying to find the right mix of chemicals to pump into me to keep me from TBBing. I scream with my real voice, and I can feel the blood in my throat from it. My face still feels like it is melting, every nerve screaming out that it is dying when it's fine, perhaps a little cold from the gel. It takes a full minute for the screaming to stop, despite trying my best. Y@@ just stares as I do so, and finally, my mind remembers what body it is in, and the screaming stops.

"Preliminary scan shows no trace of an active node," Y@@ says.

"I fucking hope so," I say in return. I am shaking, and I instinctually pat my face to see if it really is on fire.

"Do you require sedation?" Y@@ asks. It is sweet of it to think of me.

"No, no," I say. "Got anything to drink around here?"

"XyX said that you enjoy algae beer," Y@@ says. On its command, a service drone arrives with a large container, complete with a Terran style mug. "I did not know that Terrans could consume such."

"It tastes like rotten plant matter, but it sure does the job," I say as I take a large gulp. This batch is especially bitter, but it cools my throat and stomach. "Care to join?"

"Neuls are not meant to imbibe until after our optimal childbearing window closes."

"How long is that for you?"

"Seventy standard years."

"Sweetie, let me tell you, it won't hurt you or any of your little ones to just taste, especially when you aren't incubating at the moment."

"You have incubated offspring?" it asks. It sounds more sincere than usual, smelling like rich, tilled earth and blue skies. Thinking about the kids helps put the fire out in my body, if only for a moment.

"Four," I say, and then quickly add: "That's a respectable number for a Terran. We generally only birth one at a time."

"You are an exceptional combatant. I imagine your off-spring must be equally as ferocious," Y@@ says.

"My oldest, maybe, but none of them rig. I don't want this for them, never have. Unless someone convinces you otherwise, you never want your babies to hurt if they don't have to."

"Does it hurt? Incubating life? " it asks, taking a small sip from the container's straw. Diduni are big on straws.

"Sure as hell does. Every stage of it," I say, but I see it wilt a bit. "The pain is worth it, and honestly, you forget about it down the road."

"The biological machinations required to create life seem illogically complex," Y@@ says.

I think that was a joke, so I laugh.

"If I know one thing, it is that life is twice as simple as we think and ten times more complicated than we want."

The snail takes a moment and then sways a bit. "I apologize for my previous behavior."

"Not a problem. It happens. Terrans really are sentients after all"

"I do acknowledge and express shame for thinking contrary," Y@@ says. I smell tartness yet with a promise of sweet at the end. The snail takes a larger sip from its straw. "Do you have a primary mate or several?" It asks after some time.

"Just one."

"We are socially designed to be monogamous in our triads as well. It seems strange to think about."

"Can I ask something personal?" I ask, but I don't give it much of a chance to respond. "Your family told you to do this. I take it they'll tell you who to breed with?"

"Yes," Y@@ says. I smell loneliness, sorrow. It is a dusty smell, not rotten but fecund perhaps. It is both rich and enveloping, repulsive yet familiar.

"Figured. That's some heavy gravity to be sure," I say. "No way out, huh?"

"I would not self-terminate my life."

"Not what I meant." I laugh. "I mean, can't you just, not do that? I've never asked, but, I mean, this is all social requirements and expectations, not legal, right?"

"There is no legal statute that dictates I must obey my family's obligations, no."

"So you can just walk away if you want."

"Terrans can do this? You can ignore your entire cultural and social mores if you so wish? And find peace with such a decision?"

"Yep." I laugh and take a drink. "Hell, I think that's part of being Terran at a certain point."

"Fascinating," Y@@ says before moving back to a walkway. "We must discuss more while we travel."

I raise my glass and drink heavily before settling back in. I could have a different pod for the ride home, but a pod is a pod.

Y@@ and I spend much of the time talking, and the poor thing is both enamored with the idea of walking away from its pre-determined life and terrified. By the time we return to the station where my little ship is docked, it seems relatively set on its path.

"Thank you, Nora," Y@@ says as I prepare to disembark. "Your counsel proved surprising but highly effective."

"Stay well, Y@@," I say. "You're young. Never forget that you can learn from mistakes, but you can't ever get back time lost. "With that, I leave and I board my tiny ship.

The ship was once part of a prison fleet, a small boarding vessel designed to allow a single team of enforcers entry into a ship, but the crew compartment is mostly gone now, replaced with more engine. It can't go very fast, but it is sturdy, and it is reliable, and it has just enough pods for me and my family. That's why I bought it.

The slow trip home is the hardest. I burst home to let them know to expect me. For just under a standard week, it is me alone in the void. Being plugged into a rig helps ease the pain as I can pretend that I am the ship. I am steel. I am ceramic. I am dead. My body still hurts, and every time I close my eyes, all I feel is the fire on my face, the phantom sensation of legs no longer attached to my body but somehow still there.

I think back to how many times I've yelled at my children, how many times I've almost struck them with the back of my hand. I think about how scared they are of me. I've died so many times, it helps to remember what it feels like to almost die instead.

We were on a mission, border skirmish. Our carrier group was supposed to be backline, making sure no one popped through the Gate and into the main battle. I was rigged into a surveillance cruiser at the furthest stretches of the group, so far out it was like flying a ghost. The interface had a finite range, and I was skirting it, mostly lost in the millions of different data points being pumped into my brain. It was easy work, and I think Shaun browbeat me into it because we were on the rocks, and from what I had heard, he had taken a straw poll to demote me from the crew and lost. That made him bitter. It was lonely work. I was too far out to be able to sync with the others, so if I wanted to share information, I had to have the ship do it. It was easier to ignore it all, float in the sweet dark of the void, and wait.

Then I felt it, the pulse of reality being warped and bent. The ships near the Gate detected it, and within moments, a small carrier group emerged. I focused on the chatter. It was a carrier, but it appeared like a civilian freighter with private security, not an uncommon sight. The Refactor in charge hesitated, waited to see what the small fleet would do. It sent out the right hails, declaring non-combatant status, seeking safe passage to its destination. I couldn't scan that far out, but I knew, I knew it was wrong. I could feel the ships, and they all felt heavy on radiation and ammunition. They were loaded for war, the short and deadly kind.

The civilian group began to move away, keeping a respect-ful distance from our carrier, but then their engines flared and their fighters launched. They were waiting to be in the thick of us, making most of our firing solutions suicide. They were not trying to line up anything but a run on the carrier, and once the fighters and landers were out of their own carrier, the battle group went dark and broke formation. It was a hit job.

I broke my connection and bounced back to the comm dome.

"XyX, get me a fighter," I said with my real voice, trying to orient myself. The ship was already shaking from several hull breaches. The fighters were pumping out a lot of interference, and our comms were fuzzy.

"Attempting to," XyX said as loud as he was able. "We have been struck with some kind of nanite virus. My terminal is locking up."

"Upi tek," I said. I started to pull off my tethers. Before I did, I made sure to scream into the neural interface to everyone else. "Eject! We got snowies, and we got them now."

"It could be borrowed ammunition," XyX said, but I could tell he was running the math. One of his hands was already at the other command terminal, unlocking the small weapon's locker in the back of the dome. I was already there, barely in my jumper. I got a rifle ready, a breather on my face, and heavy gravboots on before any of the others were even out of their rigs. Shaun looked at me.

"Don't call for eject unless you have fucking confirmation, Nora!" Shaun screamed. He was still wired in. "Your hysteria is costing us right now! "Several of the others were already mid sprint to the locker stop, my cousin Marcus, his wife Lauren, her brother. They were all geared up, but the others were waiting for Shaun's orders. "Everyone, get back inside the rigs and get fighting!"

"Get into the defense vestibules and be ready," I said, and I was moving to the small ramparts that appeared from the floor. XyX was already in his command bubble, a mixture of liquid metal and ceramics. It looked like a floating silver orb with several large weapons protruding from it.

"Shaun, if you will not exit, I must at least seal your rigs," XyX pleaded. He smelled like salt and tasted like starch.

Shaun waved his hand and laid back down into the soup. Four others joined him. The rest exited and made their way to the locker. A hole the size of three tall men side by side opened up in the wall, and the oxygen rushed out. Everyone with a breather and heavy gravboots or inside a sealed rig survived, but six didn't, freezing and boiling at once. Once the atmosphere was gone, the pull stopped, and the outer wall opened as a lander covered it, an insect-like ship with a belly that opened to a crew department.

I had seen Upi before, but never like this. They were in their full battle suits, not even tethering. The carrier they had wouldn't support it anyway. They were here to do one thing and one thing only, and they didn't expect to live. The four floated inside, and their first instinct was to shoot the rigs. I saw the neural fluid and the blood rise up as each round found something, and I felt the cold of the void even through the heat membrane that covered me from the breather.

I opened fire, and their attention shifted. We have the ramparts to shield us, but we are outgunned, and all of our fire only downed one. Their armor was too thick, and they were using hard rounds, unafraid of damaging the ship, and we were using sonic weapons, much less reliable against their armor. A piece of metal penetrated the rampart in front of me, and I recognized the feeling of sundered flesh. This time it was real. This time it did not go away when I blinked hard. I saw blood, a lot of red globules floating away, and the pain didn't listen to me when I told it to quiet. It raged even harder, and my arms felt heavy despite the lack of air pressure.

I fell, attempting to keep my intestines from spilling out, but also seeking better cover. Then I felt the thunder of XyX's weapons firing, and half the damn room seemed to dissolve. The three Upi turned to cover, but the liquid metal formed into shields while the guns moved to fire at perfect angles. The Upi didn't last long, especially since Marcus and Lauren were still alive. The two fired into the flanks of the Upi. Then they were just dead forms.

"Terran military jargon for identify your condition!" XyX commanded.

Marcus and Lauren hailed. I couldn't hear how many people in the rigs were still there. "Nora?!"

"Here," I managed. The pain was so much I couldn't do more than whisper or scream. A fresh wave crashed into me and then I was back to screaming. Marcus rushed over to me with an aid kit, a polymer designed to push my insides back inside. It burned, burned like a fighter caught in a plasma arc. I took the med pack and injected myself with the pain killers, twice. I felt nauseous and dizzy, but it didn't matter. I was no longer screaming.

"We still have hostile attack craft, but the lander seems frozen here for the time," XyX said. "I've summoned medical and security drones. They'll be here shortly."

"Help me into a rig. Won't matter if a fighter lands a clean shot on us," I said. XyX's security dome unraveled so I could see him. Even with the eye stalks, I knew pity when I saw it.

"Don't. The stress will terminate your life."

"No, the Upi are going to kill us all if I don't," I said. With that Marcus lifted me up and placed me into the last functioning, free pod. It hurt like hell to interface, my meat already in distress, already trying to remind me that I was dying, and I was only speeding up the process.

XyX loaded me immediately into an interceptor, and I was screaming through the void, staying within meters of our carrier, trying to stay off scans and looking to stop any strikes on the domes. Three more domes were down, and even though none of them had any Terrans in them, the attacks were getting closer. There were several bombers en route, and they looked ready to pound whatever dome was left. The Upi ignored our dome since the lander was there. They had to have known their squad inside was dead, but maybe XyX managed to block their comms.

I strafed across the three bombers, fragging two instantly, but one was only clipped, and it was going for a crashdown right at a dome. I flipped the interceptor, feeling the tension of the metal, and some part knew that my Terran meat was suddenly convulsing and bleeding faster at the strain, even if it was just sitting in a vat goo. The meat was dumb; it could not help it. Thankfully, my nervous system kept the heart pumping, and the interceptor was faster than the bombers, so I managed to catch up to it and push it off course, both of us colliding and disintegrating into the carrier's hull.

I woke up coughing, more and more strands of red staining the goo around me. I couldn't speak, but XyX knew what to do. Before I stopped coughing, I was in another interceptor, hunting down the last of the Upi ships. We barely had any little birds in the air, and the Upi knew it. They were scarring up the carrier as badly as they could. Most of the ship's point-defense was focused on protecting the domes, so they switched tactics to cause enough ruptures for the whole ship to fail. Shaun was still alive and still flying, but he was mostly useless, off trying to find the Upi carrier as if that mattered. Chances are, the carrier was crewed by a whole host of other sentients, and the Upi's just caught a ride to do what they do. Killing the little birds was all that mattered, keeping the rest of us alive.

Lauren was back flying, but her rig was damaged and couldn't handle full neural interface, so she was on VR. This made her slow, and she was normally a solid flier. Still, she knew what to do, and rather than try to engage the fighters and bombers muzzle to muzzle, she herded them toward the point-defense or to me.

There were a few other ships in the void with us, but most of the domes were on lockdown, and all but the Terrans were hiding in secure areas. Richard at least made himself as useful as possible, assisting XyX with the point-defense. They'd fire in different vectors and when Lauren or I engaged, the point-defense would suddenly shift, often shredding all involved, but we had plenty of ships, and the Upi were dwindling.

The harsh reality was that the Upi were not tethering; they were actually flying. Their carrier was likely hauling ass as fast as possible, hoping that they weren't ID tagged. The Upi couldn't replace their losses, but they weren't trying to. They just wanted to kill us. I could appreciate that kind of hate; it drove so many of us for so long. They were not trying to live, just trying to die slow enough to kill us too.

It didn't matter in the end. There were not enough.

It was XyX's idea. The other frigates in the battle group moved close to the carrier, and after some math on XyX's part, he correctly calculated how much more the Carrier could take. The frigates unleashed their own point-defense against our hull, and the rest of the Upi were shredded, and our Carrier was still there, limping, useless if the battle far away turned or if we were hit by another Carrier, but still there.

I don't remember getting pulled from the rig or being placed inside a hospital pod. I don't remember who was there with me, who prayed over me, who sat there, waiting for the machines to respool the pieces of me I was missing. I just remember waking up to XyX, sitting there, idly reading through something.

"I expect gratitude for classifying this whole ordeal to be billed as extreme hazardous risk beyond obligation," he said. I tried to laugh, but it hurt so damn much. He put one of his hands on my arm to quiet me. "Would you care for more medicinal narcotics?"

"Load me the fuck up."

"You should have informed me prior to this engagement that you were pregnant," XyX said, and I detected judgment. It smelled like old copper and thick cloth.

"I figured that we took the back rank job might have been an indication," I replied, barely conscious in the physical sense. The meat was in pain, and my meat was flooded with chemicals to suppress that pain, and that filtered back to the mind. "Is the baby ok?"

"She is fine, although we estimate some severe psychological imprinting from so much stress while in utero"

"Well, ain't that true for us all?" I tried to laugh, but XyX did not find it funny.

Shaun finally came to see me, all puffed up.

"You could have killed our child, Nora," he fumed. "I told you to stay at the Reloc!"

"You and a whole lot of others would be dead if I stayed, so a thank you is in order," I shot back. Fighting with Shaun was a regular occurrence, but nothing sobered me up faster.

"The King of New Eden is expecting a match for his youngest son, and he isn't going to want some half-insane, stunted runt," Shaun seethed. That was his latest idea for increasing our grandeur, arranging marriages for Hera, Estelle, and then, before she was even born, little Maya. I wasn't having it, and nothing was signed but his empty words, but then, we hadn't sorted it out entirely ourselves either.

"None of my babies will ever marry someone cause you told them to, and that's a fact," I snapped back. Despite the chemicals in my system to keep me calm, I felt like I was back in that interceptor, ready for blood and pain.

"Shut your dumb mouth, at least in front of the snail," Shaun shouted.

XyX cocked his eye-stalks to the side. "My species have no social conditioning around marital strife. Arguments are meant to be had in public to ensure an accurate record of the incident," XyX said.

I couldn't help but laugh.

"He stays," I said, and I tried to calm myself. I wanted to hit Shaun, hit him until my fists couldn't take it anymore. "You need to leave."

"We are not done with this conversation," Shaun declared. I could see his fists tightening. I always knew when he was trying to work up the courage to do something.

XyX moved between us.

"She requested with force that you depart," XyX said.

"We are not finished with this, Nora," Shaun yelled.

"Fuck you, we are finished. Go run your ass back to whatever girl is dumb enough to buy your bullshit. Don't you ever come near me and mine again, or so help me, you'll be praying that the Upi got to you first," I screamed. I started to unplug myself from the pod. He took off before I even swung a foot out.

"Nora, I do not wish to be indecorous..." XyX started. I motioned for him to keep going as I lowered myself back into the pod. "Shaun did actively refuse my orders so he could pursue the carrier. This is grounds for the termination of his contract with the Diduni and a censure notice added to his Convocation file."

"Then do it," I said, and it felt good to say it. "I cannot expel him from the *Bondea* as we are equal partners by the contract, but I can dissolve it." It took me a moment to understand it all. There would be a lot of legal fights in the Convocations, a lot of energy, a lot of my spirit, but it did not matter. "The *Bondea* is gone. You can go ahead and begin the process."

"I understand," XyX said as he started to shuffle off. "Get your rest. I have ordered transport for you back home."

"I appreciate you," I said, and XyX made a sign with his fingers.

I didn't rig for a year after, and I spent most of my free time responding to the numerous legal bursts that came with dissolving the *Bondea*. My marriage took only a firm handshake and some side eye with the Alderman, and Shaun took his shit, his old junker ship, and left the Reloc. He didn't even bother to kiss the kids goodbye. As far as I know, that was the last time they had ever heard his voice.

Not a day goes by that I don't kick myself for not dumping him sooner. Richard and Estelle didn't take it too well, but they adapted, and Hera, well, I think Hera was honestly happy. Shaun kept pushing her and pushing her to get implants to rig, and she would not have it. He praised her more than I did. He was always the fun one, but when they fought,

I wouldn't see one of them for at least a week. She never thanked me, but Hera didn't hold it against me, and that was enough.

Thinking about Shaun helps ease the pain. He had caused me plenty, but with him gone, it doesn't hurt anymore. It is just me, the kids, Mama, and Mag, and that's enough. Flying home to them is hard though. My body hurts, but it hurts more to know that I have to change. In the void, I am Nora, the Terran ITC. I am respected. I am feared. At home, I am both, but it hurts there. It's not how it should be. Maybe I need to let go.

Part of what I hate about going home, especially now, is that I am still bitter. The rock was supposed to be just for us, a place to hide away until I was dead and the girls could take what they needed and either stay or make their own way in the world. I am still so mad at Mama for convincing me. Just thinking about it all makes the pain come back, makes the fire burn my skin down to the bone. Maybe part of it is because I know she's right and I'm wrong, but I am tired of being wrong.

I can't help but be lost in my thoughts alone in the vacuum. I can't help but revisit things. I can't help but hold my grudges close because out in infinity, that's all I have left.

When the Convocation tribunal ship entered the atmosphere of our Reloc, most went into the bunkers that we had built. The bunkers wouldn't do much besides prolong our death in the case of an Upi raid, but sometimes, it felt good to do something futile in the face of the inevitable. I wasn't too concerned, and I tried to tell the others to expect such, but panic is panic, and most of us on that rock had gotten kicked so hard and so often, you couldn't help but cower at first blush. Still, we were humans, so if the cowering didn't work, then we went with the teeth.

The Convocation did not bother to send a lander down, just dropped in a Comms-Hub for me. Instantaneous communication across the galaxy was expensive, so I was surprised by it all. I guess they really didn't want me on the ship, so they'd rather risk sending down their Hub for me to loot. Not that we would. True Convocation tech was far ahead of anything we could understand. We'd likely only use it for an outhouse.

When the Comms-Hub landed, I received a short burst with entry instructions. I gave the password, let it scan me, and then I entered, Mama watching. They wouldn't let her in, and frankly, she would not have handled it well.

Inside, there was the gentle glow of screens and neural interfaces of all varieties. I took the one that I recognized as Terran compliant, and let it crawl over me. It was like being in a rig, but I still felt my body and understood its presence in space. There was no inertia gel or anything. It was slightly dizzying to stand and be suddenly in a pitch-black nothingness, no floor, no horizon, only darkness.

I could see myself, and my clothes fell away until I decided what I wished to project. The conservative approach would be to wear my standard ITC jumper, complete with all the various awards and recognitions. This would add an air of respectability, a certain ethos of a consummate professional that was simply seeking fair commerce. That would be the wisest choice by most of the calculus, but I knew the Convocation. I knew them much better than that.

I went with full battle-gear, or what was Terran battle dress when Terra still existed. A heavy hauberk of plastics and Kevlar, a hand painted mural of Santa Mort, the last true patron deity of Terra. In one hand, she held a massive sickle, blood gently falling like her single tear out of a brilliantly brown eye. In the other, she held Terra itself, its oceans and continents intact. She stood above the broken remains of the Upi's home world and their colonies, debris littered around her feet. Her blood red lips were in a cruel smile, and her hair, much like mine, was a predator's mane, queenlike and tightly locked. I took on her own visage, a killer, an image banned in most Convocation space. The Convocation never saw us as members, so there was no point pandering to an empty illusion. It was better to leverage their fear.

"ITC-Terran 07041620," a voice sang in my skull. "Are you ready to make your statement?"

"I am," I said. Suddenly, the darkness retreated, and I stood in a room surrounded by a thousand different sentients. The translators didn't take in the gasps or non-verbal signs of distress at my appearance, but there was still a raw energy to it, the currents of emotion that even the tech can't hide.

"ITC-Terran 07041620," the same voice sang out. "We are not inclined to accept your terms."

"Well, that ain't a surprise, so you tell me why, so I can tell you why you may just be wrong," I said with a certain flourish of defiance .I couldn't be too aggressive because I didn't hold any power here, but I couldn't be demure. That didn't work with them.

"The current celestial body assigned for relocation and re-population is sufficient to your needs." The translator made all the voices sound the same, which was standard protocol for any meeting of an official body of the Convocation. All sentients are equal, after all. A truly skilled xenobiologist would be able to tell you what was speaking based on the tics in the translator, but that wasn't me.

"If you review the data pack that I sent, you'll see that our population is at negative growth, and our mortality rate is 3 Szkekian's standards of deviation above the norm and 2.3 Luzzite standard deviations above the norm," I said, and before I could be cut off, I gave a bit of a laugh, "And before you say it, no, only .03% of those deaths have been the result of bloodshed or malevolence. The leading cause of death is treatable illness due to poor atmosphere and diet"

"This is true," a voice says. "The math is correct."

"So if the math is correct, then it would lead me to believe that no, the celestial body is not at all sufficient."

"Medical supplies seem to be insufficient as well," the same voice added. I liked it. Didn't know who or what, but at least it said something like logic. I always hated having to go that route, but most of the Convocation sentients loved to tout their dedication to logic and reason, mostly as a way to hide their own emotional justifications for their actions. There wasn't anything scarier than a sentient that tried to use a veneer of mathematical precision to hide their moral failings.

"Then the Convocation can send more aid."

"Or, you could accept my offer."

"It appears unwise to allow a sizable population of Terrans to leave the surveillance and security of the Convocation."

"The new location would be registered with the Convocation as is standard agreement in any Convocation space. You are fully within your legal rights to establish a surveillance object in our orbit. The only change would be that the administration of the colony would not be under the Convocation's Bureau of Displaced Sentients but rather under our own."

"How then could the Convocation ensure a peaceful re-population as well as ensure proper security?"

"You already don't, as demonstrated in the data," I said.

There is a pause as the translators work to keep the dis-agreement from my ears. After a good chunk of time, the translator kicks over again.

"There is substantial cost in your proposal."

"So, you agree with the initial basis of the proposal?" I laughed.

More silence.

"Yes."

"So what does the Convocation feel is fair in terms of balancing cost?"

"The celestial body in question is already owned by you, but the Colony Vessel is of considerable expense."

"You are saving expense in the long run, so consider it an investment."

"No. Initial cost must be offset."

"Fine. How does 10% of the ship sound?"

"75%"

"20%"

"65%"

"15%"

More silence after that.

"50%. Final offer."

"30% and I will offer two contracts free of charge to a member state of the Convocation that covers the shortfall."

"The Diduni accept this offer," the voice returned. "It is settled. Within three hundred standard days, a Colony Vessel will arrive. You will have three hundred days after such to vacate the celestial body. You will also be billed the expense of this meeting."

With that, the darkness returned, and then real light generated by an actual star, came into the hub as the doors opened. The system disconnected itself, and once I was out, the doors sealed shut. The Comms Hub powered its small engines, and departed our rock. Well, it wasn't our rock anymore. We had a new one, at least I had one that I had to now share.

"Well?" Mama asked, waiting with the kids. Most folk were still hiding.

"They took their toll, that's for sure," I said, still a bit angry at it all. "And I'll be busy, but the deal is done."

Mama hugged me tight, and I could feel the wetness of her eyes as she buried her face into me.

"Thank you, baby," she whispers. "Hardest thing in this world is to carry people with you, not just leave em behind."

"Certainly expensive to do," I said.

That night, the colony had a celebration, and while most were singing my praises, I sat outside, staring into the night sky. I had worked plenty of jobs, but never for free. I could only wonder what the Diduni were going to do to me, knowing they wouldn't have to pay me a thing in return.

"You should be over there, basking in very deserving accolades," Mag said as he sat down next to me. He had a large mug of cold, sweet honey beer. The Beekeeper, Wythe, was an ornery sort of man, and he knew how damn precious his concoctions were. They were just about the only trade good our colony had outside of ITCs. Folk were really appreciative if even Wythe could give up some of the good stuff for a night.

"Never been a big fan of parties," I said, and it was true. There was something about groups of people, the expectation to be happy, the expectation to smile and laugh. It never sat right with me. Not that I didn't enjoy myself, but too often, I felt the weight of other eyes on me, waiting for me to be what they wanted rather than hoping to learn who I was.

"Well, here's to you anyway." Mag laughed. We clinked our mugs for a moment, and he smiled at me, that broad, wide smile that took up too much of his face. "I heard that you contracted yourself out as part of the deal."

"I did. Only way to cover the cost of the damn Colony ship," I said, trying to avoid his gaze. He hadn't looked at me that warm in a while. "I'll be getting a burst in a few days at most. The Snails have been pretty aggressive lately, trying to capitalize on everything."

"What everything?" Mag asked, taking a deep drink of his own lesser beer.

I motioned to us, to the settlement, to the stars.

"Oh."

"The Snails don't do things fast, but when they start doing it, you better get out of the way. To them, the whole ordeal is still a current event. Their perspective on time is a bit skewed, but that tends to happen when you live several centuries by our counting."

"You know them well," Mags said.

"Worked with them a fair bit," I said, looking at my drink. "I know one pretty well at least. Doubt they'll put me with him this time though. If they don't have to pay me, they'll send me to places they wouldn't send him."

"Well, I'm sorry for that, too."

"Too?"

"I know you didn't want to take anyone else. I know this wasn't your idea, but now you lose your hideaway, and have to go out there and suffer even more."

"It ain't suffering. I like what I do, and that's the simple truth," I said as I drained the honey beer. Maybe I should have savored it, but I didn't see much point in that.

"You may like it, but that doesn't mean you don't suffer either."

"Look, I appreciate that you care, and I really appreciate you taking on the kids when I'm in the black, but you don't know me."

"I'd like to," he countered. His directness caught me off guard. It was nice to see it out of him, only in the sense that he had earned it. Men were usually direct with me, but that directness was more of a demand, not a form of honesty, not a form of vulnerability.

"Well, you'll get your chance. We'll be stuck on a much smaller rock, but at least it will be ours," I said.

"Yours," Mag said with a smile.

"No, not quite," I said before I kissed him for the first time.

We didn't have a name picked out yet. Hera wanted to call it Sanctuary, but that wouldn't work. It wasn't a safe place after all. Mama wanted to call it Nu'Vo-Tee, but it certainly wasn't Terra and it certainly wasn't new. Geologically, the planet was a good eight billion years old, which made it tectonically stable. It was a small planet, really a planetoid, but it had 1.06 Terran gravity thanks to a solid lead core. While it lacked enough oxygen to have robust liquid water and breathable atmosphere, it was minerally rich, and the atmo would only take a generation of terraforming rather than ten. Its rotation around its sun meant reasonable seasons, and while the days were only half of a Terran day, it just meant you got a good nap.

Since technically I owned the rock, I got to name it, and I called it Dandara. I always liked that name. I don't think a home needs anything more than that.

4. Home

I had already dropped about a dozen eon-engines on the rock when I first bought it. They were old tek, nothing fancy, but after four standard years, they made the planet about a degree warmer on average. The nights were still lethal half of the year, so early shelters had to be reinforced or underground, but with the full Atmo-Engines from our camp, real, breathable air was not a distant hope, but a patient eventuality. The bonus to the eon-engines was that they were coded for Terran physiology, so they implanted billions of microbes that were healthy for Terran life, something our own Engines didn't have.

The Colony Ship helped the most. Without it, there was no way to take the Atmo-Engines off world, transport the agridomes, or even keep most of the livestock alive for several standard years. It also came with another two Atmo-Engines, which was absolutely necessary. With our three, it would take roughly five years to get a breathable atmosphere, and five years frozen meant most of our livestock would die and probably a good third of our population. The Colony Ship could maybe sustain our population for a year once thawed, but then the math was still brutal about when to unfreeze and when to land. Having two more engines meant we had a workable atmosphere in three years; two years on ice, one year on the ship. That was manageable.

We had to rely on luck to some extent, and that was the hardest part. Mama called it faith; I called it desperation. If any of the Atmo-Engines died, then we were going to lose people to the freeze. If we ran into bandits or anyone else looking to make some easy trade by taking a Colony Vessel, we couldn't defend ourselves. The Twins—my cousins on my Daddy's side—and Mag had managed to get some basic sat-defenses ready, but they wouldn't put up much of a fight. We outfitted the dozen or so landers from the Colony Ship with whatever weapons we could jury rig, but they weren't going to stand up to much of anything. We just had to take the chance.

I stayed awake the whole time. I had to pilot the ship and I wanted to oversee everything. It only took us a few standard months to get there, taking the most circuitous route that I could dream up just in case anyone was looking for us, but it was the terraforming that took time. Mag, the Twins, and a few other engineer types were the first to be thawed. They had the easiest time, only taking a day or so to acclimate back to the living. With them, we started the detachment process and dropped down a temporary hab and the guiders for the Atmo-Engines. Once the guiders were in, we brought down the Atmo-Engines and booted up as many technical drones as the Vessel had.

It took about two weeks to get everything going, during which I wasn't that useful. I could tell a drone what to do, but to do what I didn't know, so I spent most of my time back up on the ship, waking people up, helping them back to operational. The oldest were first, most likely to die from an extended freeze. Then the children, most likely to be discombobulated by the whole ordeal. Their meat and their mind had yet to fully connect, so the mind being truly free for months on end could be hard. The rest, those not too young or too old, had to stay on ice for a while.

There was plenty to do without worrying about the people. With the Atmo-Engines up, we had to drop down the production bay of the vessel. We had foundations to dig, underground settlements to build, and of course, agri-domes for the crops and animals. At least the Convocation didn't give us the cheapest vessel possible; the bay had a decent sized spooler, so we were able to start printing animals. Of course, they didn't give us any DNA schematics, but why would they?

I picked the spot well though. Maybe it is bravado, but I did a good job with that. The system was far from any Gate, but it wasn't so far that we'd have trouble getting to and from places. We were technically in Kxyk space, but those bugs were more concerned with their complicated system of banking and general production to care about territory. They had survived for thousands of years by being more or less war averse, rarely giving up territory and never seeking to gain any, so there was little reason for any armed conflict in their space. The system had a massive gas giant that kept asteroids in check, and it had an asteroid field that had all the basic minerals we would need.

Some ten thousand souls living on my rock, and I know that I should feel proud of what I had done to make it happen, but by my math, I had probably killed more than that. People at least said thank you, and my family wanted for nothing. We were always the first in line for a new spool of chickens, got first pick of any luxury items, and Mama was technically the Alderman of the planet now. Still, coming home always hurt. Everyone had something to do but me.

Mag was always fixing something. The kids were studying, and they each had found their passions. Hera was deep into terraforming and spooling, and Mag kept feeding that. Richard and Estelle loved working with the animals, and they were pretty good at it all told. Maya was too young to really have a choice, but Mag always said that she built things that no five year old should build, so I guess she imprinted on him pretty solid. Even my extended family were busy.

My oldest nephew, Mikail, was the ice hauler. My brother, Samuel, hadn't lived to see the boy reach anything like manhood, but if Samuel was out there, somewhere, he would be proud. Mikhail could pilot about as well as anyone, and he had a knack for finding the asteroids with that perfect ratio of stability and frozen H2O. Our orbital processing center always had a queue of rocks ready for it. By the time we made full landfall, we had several billion gallons of clean, fresh water stored on the planet, and we were already starting to dump the excess into what would eventually become our world's ocean. I doubt I will live to see it, but one day, maybe Maya will be fishing that ocean, bringing up the descendants of the embryos we had saved.

If she did, that'd be mostly Hera's doing. She had been studying hard in her genetics, and she had already spooled out several extinct Terran creatures. We had rabbits and guinea pigs because of her, and she wasn't bad at thinking the long game. She had spooled out trout and catfish for our aquafarms, mostly out of what data we still had. She had to cheat a bit, and they weren't genetically perfect recreations, but they were close enough, and that's all we needed. We could live on close enough. As much fight as she had in her, it wasn't hard to see that she was smarter than she was angry, and that was a blessing. Made her better than me at least.

The Twins were already solid engineers, but they were growing fast too. They were always working on something, and whenever I came back from a long haul in the void, they'd have something new up and running. To keep them busy, I once told them to build a full Comms hub out away from the township, just in case we ever wanted anyone landing with something heavy, and it only took them a standard year to get something workable up. Those two cried real nighttime story tears when they first saw the Colony Vessel's drone system, and with that much muscle to do the work, all they really had to do was think.

Mama organized folk, got us working like a real town, not that I had ever seen one. As much as I had been all over the stars, I mostly saw Carriers and warships, not spending time on planet unless I was blowing something up. That felt more like home than walking around trying to determine if a plant was a weed or something edible. It was strange interacting with people without the general understanding that we were likely about to die, about to suffer, about to cause suffering. There was a closeness that came from that but also a distance. You knew that there was always an out waiting, and if the friendship soured, in the end, it'd be over sooner than you'd think. That wasn't true at home.

Part of what hurts is that when I am out in the town, people don't look at me like I'm there. They either stare or pretend they aren't staring. Granted, Hera and I have had some pretty big blowouts publicly, and Hera still has the reputation of a firebrand. The poor Jackson boy lost an ear to her. She said he was getting too familiar, and he said that she was leading him on, but most people just thought of me when they thought of her and figured we were just like that. Ungrateful, I say. Doesn't matter what you do for folk, they'll always find a way to put you beneath them. Still, I couldn't just sit at home all day. I'd go insane being underground. I was meant for big spaces.

I am getting closer now, only a day out, and now able to pick up the encrypted signals of our bare bones sat-system. Reaching out with the scanners, I detect the tiny pulses of Mikhail's ice hauler, going out for another run into the belt. I feel a jolt of adrenaline when I detect a new signal, a larger vessel, and by instinct, the few weapon systems I have are on and the engine is already powering up for combat or a glorious end.

It takes a second to calm the heart once the scanners confirm that it's a merchant vessel, complete with all the usual ID tags. Someone came by to trade at our tiny spaceport, set up closer to the belt where our planet's twin, a lifeless hunk of stone, mostly blocks ours. We need trade, but I don't want to advertise. Mag convinced me that a small spaceport would be fine, mostly drone operated, and if the Upi came calling, they'd hit that first and give us a chance to dig in or run .I hope they brought something worthwhile.

I cut the engines back and take the more lackadaisical approach home. I miss my family, but I am not ready to go back just yet. The void has a pull on the soul, and my head still feels like it is burning half the time. I haven't managed much sleep. I dream about running in that beast again. It felt good to run, to be simple, to be free.

I come into orbit as the sun begins to rise. The Comms hub is working like a charm, and I land without issue. There's no party waiting. The air is still lethally cold at this hour and season, but the winds are calm. I unplug and then suit up. Thankfully, the little motorized bike that Mag built is still waiting for me just a quick walk from the landing pad, housed in a tiny, insulated shed. It starts right up, and through the suit's oxygen exchange, I can smell him on it. No doubt he stopped by not that long ago to make sure it was working.

There is a fine layer of snow on the ground, honest to goodness frozen precipitation, and I smile.

I ride the bike down the hastily built road, and it is my last calm before the storm. I breathe deep, trying to focus. I am here. I am alive. The meat is fine. I am not the meat. I am this meat.

The steel doors leading down into our hab are freshly painted. It's mostly Estelle and Richard's handiwork, but I can see a few handprints from Maya, handprints far bigger than I remember. I see the careful, delicate linework of Hera. It is a lovely welcome home banner, and part of me fills with a warmth that is hard to quantify, and another part of me is full of a self-hate for not giving as much of a shit as I should.

I punch in our code. The doors slide open, and I walk inside. When I get to the inner doors, there is another decoration for me, and this one is definitely Mama's handiwork. It is a letter, telling me to think right, act right, and try to stay calm at Hera. Mama knows.

Once inside the inner doors, I can take off the suit, and real, actual heat fills me. I smell food cooking, and my body is hungry. The ship's rig keeps the body nutritionally fed, but my stomach is actually empty and has been for a few weeks now. I smell cooking flesh, and for a moment, my face is on fire again, my legs give out and I nearly stumble to the ground. I breathe deep, bite my lip to feel a little bit of real, not shadow, pain.

Mag is in the cutout designed to be a kitchen, cooking something over the stove. We have a real pressure system, but he likes using the fuel burning one, says it matters to the flavor of things. He's romantic about food, the alchemy of chemistry, engineering, and craft. Mama agrees, so we only use the proper systems when we need a lot of food quickly. I know he hears me, but he doesn't move because he doesn't want to rush me. I wrap my arms around him from the back and breathe deep, drinking in all the smells together.

"Hey baby, hungry?" he asks like he just saw me five minutes ago.

"You know that answer," I say.

He puts down the spatula and turns to me, kissing me deeply. I know how much he misses me by how long he lingers after a kiss, sometimes kissing me again, reminding himself of the taste.

"Got a good surprise for you. Want it cold, cool, or warm?" he asks as he gestures to the lump of protein on the preparing table. Generally, I hate cold food, but if it's meat, right now, I want it cold inside, still red, still bloody.

"Just make sure it doesn't bite me back, but I want that risk to it," I say and Mag laughs. He pulls out a hunk of meat from the oven, giving it a second to cool and cook in its own juices. It smells better than anything else in the world. He finishes scrambling up some eggs, rice and beans fried in what smells like real fat, and quick as an interceptor, I have a full plate in front of me with an extra surprise, a hot cup of real black tea.

"Now you usually don't rate high enough for this, but it is a special occasion and all," he says as he serves me, getting out some of the Wexani pepper sauce he knows I love.

"You must have fucked up big to be trying this hard to smooth things over."

"I may have sold the planet. Not sure. The translators don't work so well." He laughs. He makes himself a plate and sits down with me. I take a bite of the meat. It is cold and red inside with a brilliant ruby center, and before I know it, the steak is gone and in my stomach.

"This tastes real, not just protein."

"Real bovine, actually born too, not a spool."

"So did you really sell this rock to be able to afford this?" I am half serious, and Mag just laughs.

"No, but the Ngozi's had four calves while you were gone, and one of the cows had a bit of trouble after, so they put her down. They gave us more than a few good cuts."

"Why they do that?" I ask, again mostly serious. Mag snickers a bit and shakes his head.

"Residual payment for keeping a statistically significant portion of our species alive," Mag says, a bit more dry than he intends maybe, but he smiles, and I smile back. You can literally build people a world, and they'll forget about you soon enough, but I guess it's nice when they don't.

"How are the kids?" I ask, mostly to change the subject.

Mag nods; he knows. He takes a slow, delicate sip of the tea and smiles.

"Doing well enough," he says but his face drops a bit. "Hera hasn't been in a good space the past week. She tried to spool out something and it went bad, real bad."

"How bad?"

"It was healthy, but it wasn't right. Attacked her and the Rivera boy that was helping her. She put it down, but still, was a hard lesson."

"She's ok though, right?" Hera is tough, but still, creating a rabid meat suit has killed more than a few before, especially those trying to build more exotic fare.

"She's fine. The Rivera boy took it worse I think, lost part of his lip."

"What the hell was she trying to spool that could do that? We don't need attack animals. We need food." That sounds like Hera, some wild idea in her head that she just has to follow, and it ends up causing nothing but problems. Spooling out chickens or ducks wasn't fun, but it kept people alive.

"A feline of some type, I think as a pet for Maya," Mag says, and he knows my look. "She's been punished enough by it all, so just keep that in mind."

"Fair enough," I say and take a long sip of the tea. It'd taste better with whiskey in it. "The youngers?"

"Richard and Estelle are good, both doing well learning husbandry. They got a good touch with our animals and learn more each day. Maya is reading now, mostly sight words, but she can do it on her own."

I fight back tears at this.

"Now that is something," I say quietly. I am about to ask more before I hear the sounds of my youngest children yelling out for me, sprinting out of their alcoves and into my arms.

I spend most of the day with them attached to me, hearing all of their stories, all of their little lives that are endless and fathomless. Hera pops her head out, sees me, gives me a small smile, and then returns to her alcove. I try not to take it personally. I try.

By the time the first night of the waking day begins, I have a bottle of the cheap trade corn mash whiskey open. My body is tired and hurts. The fire is starting again, and I can't help but want to punch something open and start eating. Part of me misses the sound of bone crunching followed by the sweet tang of blood in my mouth.

Mama returns from her office, a late session negotiating with the trader apparently, but she's all smiles and hugs. She sits down with me while Richard and Estelle take their midday nap, Maya already asleep on me.

Mama looks at me with her old, almost bored eyes. They are gorgeous. I take a heavy pull from the bottle and then brush a few errant hairs out of Maya's face. Children are always angelic when they sleep. It must have been nature's way of making you forget what pricks they can be.

"Good score, both of them. Didn't think I'd live to see trade like that twice in one lifetime, let alone back to back," Mama says. She is running through her numbers, watching the auctions flash by. Still nothing worth a bid, but she believes. She believes that just once, in all probability, kindness will shine down on us, and we can score something useful at a fair price.

"I'm getting old, Mama. Getting real old, real fast," I say. My fingers still feel like they are on a hot stone. I can feel blisters that aren't there. It is getting harder and harder to shake, and even after a week away from the rig, I am still hurting.

"Ain't never older than the day you were born." Mama chuckles. "You put in work for this family. No shame in easing down, maybe focusing on the babies instead of the accounts."

"Who else is going to bring in trade?" I counter.

Mama rubs her hands, hands more tired than mine, not just in the mind but the bone.

"Your husband ain't no slouch with the repairs. He could probably pick up work on a few ports for a bit," Mama says. "He's got a good touch with reactors. Ours hardly ever fusses anymore."

"I'd rather he be here. The girls can't trade one parent for another." I drink hard again. "Especially not him for me."

"You just out of practice. In your blood after all," Mama tries to reassure me, but it doesn't work. The kids fawn over their stepfather, and for good reason. I don't doubt their love for me, but I do doubt the application of my love.

"Your cousins do alright bringing in scrap and some wages. We can get by. We're mostly self-sufficient now."

"Self-sufficient doesn't mean much if we don't have the sat-defenses in place," I say. .Mama knows I'm right. We got terraforming towers up. We got good, workable farm domes, but all it would take is one light frigate, one moderately outfitted team, and we'd be done. We survive by staying low, staying unnoticed, but that won't last forever. It never has. No one has ever survived that way. You survive by being too damn mean and too damn stubborn to die.

"There are a few that we could get now." Mama tries, every time, she tries. "Between the twins and Mags, they could get them up to snuff."

"No, Mama," I say after another good drink. It tastes like fermented shit, but it does the trick. My fingers don't feel like they are on fire anymore. "We need something reliable."

"You could reach out to some of the others too, ya know," Mama says. This is always her last argument. Always the last ditch effort. "They all know you, know you are a good one to have on their side and a bad one to piss off. We could affiliate with them all officially. Have some heat on our side."

"No." I don't mean to sound so firm, but I'm tired of it. "The Dessa have too many enemies to survive much longer, and the Isley families just roll over and show belly. All of them either want to cause mayhem or try to rebuild what is always going to be gone, and I don't have time for either of that nonsense."

"Nothing wrong with trying to get back something like home," Mama says, and I know she means it. It's different for her. She has memories of Terra. She has memories of its orange and black sky, the warm waters, the blistering summers. She had to watch it burn apart like ash, hiding in a rich man's ship. She watched them space her father, even after Terra was already gone.

"Mama, there is no reason to go back to Sol system. It's just a story men like to tell to make themselves sound big."

"That's the truth." Mama laughs. "Lord, I must have heard it so many different ways, so many different times."

"They still do it now." I laugh with her. "Walk right up to you and declare that they're going to terraform Mercury, and they're gonna make the Convocation give them a world-builder, and they are going to rebuild Terra itself out of the rocks that still float around there."

"Honestly, do they actually have those things, Nora?" Mama asks, and I forget that she's spent far more of her life on a rock than out there in the black. She's probably only met a handful of other sentients, and the stories that get passed around the comms, well, they are special.

"I don't know, Mama," I say. "Probably. Shit the Convocation has is just, it's damn near magical. Close to gods as I can tell."

"Seems like if they was godly, the galaxy be a whole lot better," Mama says. "Seems to me, if I could remake planets and cure any sickness, I'd find a way to make sure honest people got it."

"Nobody is honest, Mama," I say. "That's how we survive: remembering that nobody is honest, not even us."

Mama doesn't say much after that. I finish the bottle and get into my bed. The rock is turning back to cold, and even with the shields and the heaters, the chill can run deep through the stone. Still, warmer than it was when we first landed. The terraforming engines are working, maybe not as fast as anybody would like, but well enough for what they could afford. By the time the babies are grown, you could sleep on the surface without freezing to death. Maybe I would live to eat fruit grown in the earth of this rock, not the heavily modified soil sitting in a dome.

Mag shifts in his sleep to put his arm around me, and I breathe in his scent. I may not have the same olfactory sensors as the meat, but it still smells good. Part of me wants to wake him up, make love like we are going to die in the morning, and make this rock just a bit warmer, if only for a moment. The other part recoils at his touch, nerves trying to remember the difference between pain and pleasure. Branson, the oldest ITC I had ever met, used to say that pain and pleasure are just different sides of the same coin, and he was a rich man.

Right now, my nerves only know pain, remember the burning, every inch of my skin melting away, then the muscles, and then there was nothing but the smell. I push it all down, try to remember that I'm sleeping next to my husband, a man that took on children not his own and raised them better than me or their father. A man that never took umbrage with my work, never tried to take me down to build himself up. He's a partner, tried and true, and he loves me, loves me enough to know when to walk away and when to keep me anchored. It helps to think about it that way. It helps to remember.

He's tall but skinny, bones made from weaker artificial gravity. He arrived on the first Convocation ship that we had seen in over a standard year, barely any supplies but another few hundred mouths to feed. He and the rest of the refugees were surviving out of a small flotilla of penal ships, but the systems started to fail, and the several thousand turned into several hundred. The Convocation ships picked them up, doctored them as best they could, and dropped them off. It was a small miracle they bothered to provide the medicine so they could live in real gravity. Quarter of them died anyway.

Mama and I were already fixing on leaving, waiting for one more payment to kick in from a job before taking the babies on our little skiff and settling in on our new rock, but when we saw the newest batch, Mama was dead set on staying a little longer .She never could watch people suffer, and we were the wealthiest folk. I didn't like to show it, but we were well-fed, well-medicated, and I had four healthy babies, and that was far more than most could say.

Mag came to us when one of the terraforming towers started to sputter, putting way too much nitrogen into the atmosphere. He had the know-how, but he didn't have the parts. He didn't have any fancy Convocation schooling, but he had survived by keeping machines alive, and to his credit, he could read and read fast. His most precious item was his datapad, memory full of whatever schematics and treatise that he could mine.

"Captain Nora, is it?" he asked, not so much sheepish but rather appropriately respectful. I wasn't the leader, we had an Alderman for that, but most people knew that if you wanted something done, I would do it faster and cheaper than any official.

"What you need?" I returned. I was still stewing over Mama's decision to stay. I wanted off that rock and onto our own little nothing several billion light years away.

"I have a list of parts to fix the Atmo generator, but they aren't common," he said, unafraid to look me in the eye. "I was wondering if you might have some of them." He handed me the datapad, and the Twins took it and went through our stockpile.

"I'll see what I can do," I said. "Payment?"

"A statistically significant percentage of our species living for a few more weeks?" he responded.

I couldn't help but laugh.

"Seems fair, I guess." I didn't know what else to say. He was cute, and honestly, I hadn't much experience talking with men who weren't trying to bed me, get hired by me, or steal my job. "You can wait in the play module if you want while we sort it out. Don't mind the children; they don't bite hard."

"Give them time," he said as he walked into the small section of our habitat that was just for the kids. I figured the best way to mess with him was to let him wrestle with my four babies. I went into the stockpile to help the Twins, and by the time I came back, I expected him to be a nervous wreck in the corner or better yet, outside. Instead, there he was, sitting on the floor, playing with the dolls and spaceships that Mama and I had made.

"So how does photosynthesis work?" Hera asked. She had such a mean streak, seeing her sit with a stranger and listen to the words coming out of their mouth was absurd.

"Well, that's a long answer, but if you aren't going to be bored, we can try it together." Mag smiled. "I still don't quite get all the details myself, so you'll have to help me."

Hera was all teeth, and for a moment, she wasn't just an ITC in training. It was so hard to get her to focus on anything that wasn't running wild, but there she was, happy and content to sit still and learn.

"We got the parts," I said, maybe a little louder than I intended. Part of it was the hurt that a stranger talked with my daughter far better than I ever did.

"I'll get right on it." Mag stood and then knelt down again to shake Hera's hand. "Would you like to come? Maybe learn a thing or two about putting a machine back together?"

"Can I, Mama?" Hera asked. It was one of the first times that she had ever asked me for anything. Every other time, she whined, cried, threw a fit and demanded something, and then I'd yell right back.

"Uh, yeah," I said until the reality of leaving her alone with a strange man hit. "I'll come too, just in case."

"Of course," Mag said. He knew what I meant. He also knew how to focus Hera, how to give her tasks to help keep her engaged without sounding demeaning. He also did not try to instill any discipline, just told her when something wasn't helpful, and when he was doing the delicate work, he gave her something to do far away. I learned a lot from that. I learned how embarrassed my own Mama must have been of me. Folk always said that I should know how to be a mother, but nobody told me how to do that. Even my own Mama, at this point, she was so busy trying to keep the place running. I resented her for that. I needed help learning how to be a mother, but she was taking care of thousands of other people.

"So don't lie to me..." I started. Mag and I were drinking in the makeshift cantina in the camp. He promised to pay in exchange for the parts, but everyone knew it was him that got the engine back running, so he drank for free, and I drank for free. "How'd you know how to settle Hera down? Ask around, hardly anyone here wants to take care of her while I'm gone."

"My older brother," Mag said. "He was a hurricane like her, bad attitude, quick on his temper and faster with the language." Mag was laughing now, the kind of laugh that comes from memories that were once a source of tears but grief made them comedies. "I used to absorb a lot of it, but there was one time when our guardian, some random fool who got roped into taking us on, beat him to the point he could hardly walk. I was taking care of him, and I couldn't help but ask him why he had to fuss so much, why he couldn't just keep his head down, and this is what he said to me: 'I got pain in my blood, and nobody tells me sorry for it, even though it ain't my fault. So I'm gonna make em listen.'"

"Well, fuck."

"He was thirteen maybe? I was nine. But he was right. When I listened to him, when I gave him a chance to be what he wanted to be, that's when he could settle down, so that's all I did with Hera."

"What happened to your brother?" I asked. I didn't really want to know the answer. I knew it already, but I didn't want him to have to say it.

"Died on an Upi raid," Mag said, this time no laughter, just grief. "Joined up with a crew that had found one of their settlements. Died doing nothing but hurting other people for no other reason than he didn't know how else to handle his own hurt."

"Upi ain't people," I said.

Mag stood and put his drink down.

"They say the same about us, and that's why Terra is gone. That's why their planet and all their planets are gone. That's why we're here." With that, he gave a slight bow, and he walked away.

We didn't speak for six months after that. He was never cold to me, never harsh, and hell, he ended up teaching Hera and the Twins in engineering, but I could tell he had no interest in speaking to me.

I don't know why, but thinking about that helps me ease into the presence of his body. I push against his side, smell the dried sweat on him, and the pain in my stomach starts to ease. Maybe because even in our worst fights, when the day is the hardest, I know that he lets me speak the pain in my blood, and he listens. If anything, he listens too damn well. When we fight, he can hear my anger, but he can also hear the sadness underneath it, and then I feel a little too seen.

I manage to sleep, holding his hand I sleep dreamlessly. When I wake, he is still there, clearly awake for much longer, but letting me be comfortable. He looks at me, and when I push away, he laughs, and we start the second morning home routine.

He takes Estelle and Richard to the agri-domes, first for the livestock, then to our crops. We grow corn mostly and various tubers. Mama was real proud to have saved some dasheen from Terra, so we always have a spot for it. We are still in the process of building a dome for wetter crops like rice and quinoa, but we have enough now to start in earnest.

Mama wakes and goes into the center of town to work. Apparently, several families are feuding over breeding rights to our finest strain of goat, and Mama has been getting deeper into the Kyxk finance world, since we are technically citizens of their government, and she is working deals to get more steady trade into the planetoid.

That leaves me with Maya and Hera. Hera is easy, in some ways. She makes her own food, sets her own schedule, and Mag built her a small conveyance, so she can come and go as she pleases. She wakes up late, stays out late, and mostly stays in her alcove working on something before going to the fabrication center to spool something out. Maya is a whole other story. She is mostly content to play the various games on her console, learning her numbers and perfecting her reading, but she also has the demands for attention. I am still a novelty to her, and the reality is that I have spent more time in the void than with her, so she is hungry for me. I wish I could say the same.

I do my best, I really do. I try to keep up with the games that she spins out of her mouth at a rapid pace. I try to pretend that I am the courageous farmer, scaring away the mutated fauna that surrounds us. I try to sit and talk sweetly with her, but it's hard. I just don't have the patience. Some part of me must be broken. XyX said that constant neural interfacing could impede oxytocin production, and maybe that's it. Maybe I am just broken. Maybe I was just never meant to be a mother.

Shaun was always on me about that. I was never a good enough mother, never a good enough wife. Even Mama seems to suggest that I should just know better, but I don't. I try to be her, but it doesn't work, and maybe my meat is broken, maybe my meat was supposed to show me how to do this because of what it is. It doesn't. Maybe my mind is too used to the other tools, to the other ways of being. Maybe the meat and the mind really aren't that similar.

"Mama? Are you lookin? Are you?" Maya says as she is showing me a picture that she drew sometime ago. Looking at the vibrant reds, the splashes of orange, all I can feel is my hair starting to burn, skin liquifying on my face. I close my eyes.

"Give me a moment, baby," I say through my teeth. I want to scream at her to just shut up for a few seconds and give me some peace. I try to sip my tea, to remember that I can still taste and not just taste my nerves dying.

"Mama? Mama? I made it for you," Maya insists. Without noticing, I shatter the clay mug in my hand, also a gift from Maya. The hot tea burns my hand, the acidity in it burning the cuts as well. "Fuck!"

"Your mug!" Maya screams, and she is crying now, trying to pick up the pieces.

I leap away from her, breathing deep, trying to decide whether I grab something to clean up the tea or walk away entirely. Part of me is not really there anymore; I am back in the ship, burning myself to death. I have my burned hand in my mouth, but the pain, her voice, the memories in the flesh, they make me bite down, and now I am bleeding.

"Owwwww!"

"Baby?" I ask, suddenly back in my body, hurting but not on fire. "Baby?" Maya is holding her finger, cut on a shard, and I rush over to scoop her up. I hug her tight, and she cries. All I want to do is crush her against me and scream "Pain is life. Soak it in, let it make you strong! "Instead, I coo as best I can. When she is calm, I take a look. It isn't much of a wound, but it is to a child. Pain is universal, but it is not universally measurable.

"I'm sorry, Mama. I didn't mean to make a mess." Maya is still crying, but quieter at least.

"What happened now?" Hera calls out as she stumbles awake.

"Can I get some help here?" I ask, a little harsher than intended. Hera grumbles something, sees the mess, and grabs a compost vacuum. She sucks up the tea and the clay then dumps it into the composter chute.

"Your mug..." Maya trails off.

"You can make a new one with me," I say. "After we clean up your hand." I am still bleeding, and I've stained her little jumper. Hera takes Maya from me.

"Clean up yourself first. Blood is a bitch to clean." Hera is annoyed. I suppose she is still primarily on laundry.

"Don't use that language in front of your sister," I snap back, equally as annoyed. Hera's right, but that makes it worse.

Hera takes Maya to the medical alcove. A simple bandage and ointment and the girl is right as rain.

"Breaking things already, huh?" Hera is snide as she walks by with Maya.

I try to stuff down a response.

"Watch her for a bit," I command. "I want to see if I can get that old exo up and running finally."

"Don't bother," Hera says.

"Girl, I need that up and running in case of planetside violence, and if nothing else, it gets me a bonus on jobs when I can bring my own equipment." I had long ago bought a junked exo, mostly for Hera. Shaun pushed for it, and I could see the sense. She was a spitfire, a hellion, but those were profitable traits with the right training.

"It's gone. Besides, if Mag couldn't fix it, you sure as shit can't," Hera sneers as she says it. She never wanted to train. All she wanted to do was spool out her projects, and that cost us resources, valuable resources. Still, I always wanted to have it running, just in case.

"It better not be, that's for damn sure," I start to yell. I can't help it. "I got that for you so maybe you could start providing for the cause here." I don't mean that. That's Shaun's words coming out of my mouth.

"Well it is, so no use yelling at nobody," Hera screams back at me. "You can't make it work, and you can't make me rig in it, so why don't you just take off again like always? Life is a lot easier here without you."

There it is. The truth of it all. It hurts to hear. I can feel my skin burn again, my bones cracked from the vibrations of sonic weaponry. Inside, my heart beats in my skull, and my lungs pour emptiness into my chest.

"You ungrateful little bitch…" I start. It's too easy to start. I can't ever seem to stop it. "You play all damn day spooling out your fucking fantasies, using up what little we got, and for what? I ask you to put in work for this family and you come at me with this bullshit?"

Hera stands to her full height, just a bit taller than me, and she does not back down.

"Just leave already! No one wants you here!" Hera's spit covers my face as she says it. She puts her hands on me to push, and by instinct, I lock down on them, twist one of her wrists in a way it was never meant to twist, and I sweep out her leg. She is on the ground now, and the meat is telling me to put my foot on her throat and press hard. Training is automatic. My teeth crack against themselves. I don't even hear Maya's crying, just my teeth, the tension of Hera's joints as they start to ever so slightly fail against the pressure.

In that moment, feeling my foot want to step and step hard, feeling the meat, the pain, the memories all swirl together to make me an instrument of their wrath, the simple thought came into my head: *You don't have to be this.* My grip loosens, and Hera scrambles away and to her feet.

"Hera," I say, and my voice is a whisper. I want to scream, but I choose to be still. "I love you, Baby. I'm proud of you. And I'm sorry I'm hurting. I'm hurting real bad here. I'm sorry I spoke to you like that, sorry I put my hands on you."

"Well fu…" Hera starts, but then she stops. I understand the reflex. This has been sixteen years of her life, after all. "You shouldn't have to be sorry that you're in pain."

"But I do need to be sorry about how I use that pain." I can't stop the tears now. They are quiet things, but they drop fast. "I stay away because I'm scared. Scared you'll follow me into a rig, and then you'll have to hurt like this too. Scared I'm not good enough to do this right. Scared one day I'll hurt you because that's all I know how to do."

"I miss you, every time," Hera says, and now she is in tears. We cry the same way. No heavy breathing, no screaming, just silent water down the cheeks. "I get so mad that you're gone, and I get so mad at myself for it cause I know you're out there for us. You do this all for us."

"If I could make the resources I do here, I'd be here. I just don't know how to do anything else."

"You don't need to do more, Mama." Hera smiles, wiping her cheeks. "We got enough. We can get by."

"I'm so sorry, Hera." I bring my daughter in close. She recoils at the touch first, but her shoulders relax. "I'm so sorry I was never what you needed."

"You have always been what I need." Hera hugs me back hard. "Maybe not what I wanted, but always what I needed." With that, she dries her eyes and goes with Maya to help feed the chickens and gather the eggs for breakfast. I have to take more than a few minutes for myself.

I suit up and make the walk to our own pasture-dome. Estelle and Richard are already there, feeding the goats, checking the seals, sometimes being children and chasing the rabbits. Richard won't eat rabbit, so we usually have to lie and tell him we are eating something else, which is easy enough since most of the time, it is just protein paste, so it could be anything. Estelle, despite being younger, she'll eat whatever you put in front of her, but she'll still hold and snuggle those little lives for all they are worth. A sick part of me thinks this is good: loved meat is sweeter meat.

I am shocked to see a full, honest to the void cow in the middle of the grassland part of the dome, happily chewing its cud. The whole colony has maybe a hundred all told, and we never bothered with one since they drank so much damn water for so little. Still, made sense why the tea was so good this morning.

"Hey Mama!" Richard belts out, startling a hatch of rabbits as he runs up to me. I lift him up. It's getting a bit harder as the boy is almost as tall as me. My muscles may have forgotten, but I still remember when I could hold him in one arm and plot out a raid. "Did ya see Ollie?"

"She's certainly fine, indeed," I say. "And how did we get her?"

"While you were gone, Hera traded that old exosuit that Daddy couldn't fix for it," Estelle adds, clutching onto my leg while scanning the grass for any parasites.

"She did, did she?" And with that, I help the two with their chores. It feels good to work the soil. Richard shows me his favorite rabbit, and while I hold it, he counts out all of its various babies, several generations deep already. With the dome secured and handled, we all go back to the home for studying.

Mag is teaching a whole lecture to the kids on basic electrical engineering, and I can hear a few private bursts to Richard and Estelle from the other kids in their homes, jealous that they get to see the teacher in real life. One day, we'll finish the school, and it will be warm enough for kids to walk there.

Mama comes home to rest. I take Maya so the old woman can get a nap alone for a change. There's a small bottle with a note from Mikail's wife, Margaret: a gift from their newest crop. I crack it open and pour a glass, looking over the ITC postings. Plenty of work, a few personal invitations. I scan through the system, idly researching each one. Maya coos in her sleep, and thankfully, she always was an easy sleeper. I stroke her head and try to imagine what she is dreaming of. She has a slight smile on her face, her one dimple deep and full. It must be good. I make a few selections on the screen and I cannot help but let out a deep, low sigh.

"Hey, Snail," I say. I look at the whiskey, home grown right here, and I take a sip. Maya is gently snoring now, just like her Granddaddy used to do, and Hera is in the next alcove, studying her terraforming. She really is a natural at growing things. I clear my throat again, and I want to believe it is from the bite of the liquor. "I just officially retired. These are my personal coordinates, so feel free to drop me a message whenever. If you're ever in the X78 sector of quadrant AB8, give me a burst. You can take the grandkids to come see a real Terran homestead." I swallow the words hard, but I make them return. "It'd be nice to see an old friend."

About the Author

Daniel Jose Ruiz is an educator and writer from Los Angeles. Like most others, he can't claim LA as his birthplace; he's a transplant too, but he's been here for more than half his life, so that should count for something, right? He is a native Texan although he only lived there for a few years, but at least if he ends up back there, he can get those cool Native Texan license plates.

He is a graduate of the CalArts MFA program in Creative Writing and he is a dedicated Anteater, having earned both his BA and MA in English from UCI. He is a tenured Professor of English at Los Angeles City College, and trust me, he is damn proud to be there. He is married to the absolutely underappreciated visual artist Flavia Zuniga-West-Ruiz, and the father of the completely adorable Prometeo and the newly arrived Artemisia Chelo. He spends most of his time with them.

He is an absolute geek, and not in that ironic way that is cool right now. No, he's just a geek that loves tabletop war games like Warhammer 40,000, RPGs like Dungeons and Dragons, and video games of all varieties. He sucks now at multiplayer, which hurts his heart quite a bit.

Daniel doesn't believe in genre much, so he writes whatever comes to mind, whether that be Poetry, Science-Fiction, Fantasy, or Literary Fiction. It's all just stories to him, and he tries to tell good ones, and he tries to make sure there are brown boys, girls, and folk in between inside of them because it felt pretty lonely reading all those stories that never had them. He is an older millennial, so he sucks at the whole social media thing, but he's learning.

OTHER TITLES CURRENTLY AVAILABLE AND ON PRE-ORDER FROM